Fanny Bruce Cook

Fancy's Etchings

Fanny Bruce Cook

Fancy's Etchings

ISBN/EAN: 9783743304994

Manufactured in Europe, USA, Canada, Australia, Japa

Cover: Foto ©Andreas Hilbeck / pixelio.de

Manufactured and distributed by brebook publishing software (www.brebook.com)

Fanny Bruce Cook

Fancy's Etchings

Fancy's * Etchings

BY

FANNY BRUCE COOK.

SAN FRANCISCO:
JOSEPH WINTERBURN CO., PRINTERS AND ELECTROTYPERS,
417 Clay Street, between Sansome and Battery,
1892.

INDEX.

——:o:——

Fancy's Etchings.

WINTER.

WHO welcomes the winter?   Not I, not I,
　　Though a merry wight is he;
　Though he laughs as he hangs his sparkling gems
　　On boughs of the leafless trees;
Though like jewels the icicles gleam and shine,
　　I turn from their glist'ning rays;
From the might of his glazing breath I turn
　　To the golden summer days.

Though his brow be decked with a diadem,
　　As he waves his frostly wand;
Keep me from the chill of his freezing glance,
　　Or the clasp of his icy hand;
For I hail not the fall of the autumn leaf
　　When the shiv'ring breezes blow—
When the glad earth doffs her flowery robe,
　　For a winding sheet of snow.

Though the moon and stars wear a brighter flash
   Yet the twilight skies are pale;
Oh! give me the blush of the dewy spring,
   When the tempests cease to wail.
For I love the rills, the birds and flowers,
   The zephyr, and gorgeous beams,
That Apollo flings to the chanting waves,
   As they toss the shining streams.

Though many may welcome the Christmas feast,
   And the new year gladly greet;
Yet the poor love not the gathering frost,
   Nor the freezing rain and sleet;
As they look from their homes of woe and want,
   With boding hearts of sorrow,
As they list to the tempest's madd'ning strife,
   How they dread the dark to-morrow.

While the wild winds rush o'er the storm-lash'd main,
   And the writhing waters leap,
And the bright stars sink in the cloud-wrapped skies,
   Like snow-flakes in the deep.
Oh! they are desolate, weary and sick,
   While the rich are glad and gay;
God pity the lot of the hapless crowds,
   That are striving from day to day!

Would you think it a season of joy for them,
   And call it a bright New Year—

With a mouldy crust for a Christmas feast,
   And their New Year's gift—a tear?
Then who hails the winter?   Not I, not I,
   Though a merry wight is he;
Though he laughs as he hangs his sparkling gems
   On the bough of the leafless tree.

CHILNUALNA.*

Hail me, dashing Chilnualna!
   O'er the cliffs and crags I'm leaping;
Where the wild Bear, and the Lion,
   From their lairs are stealthy creeping.

Here I love to shout and clamber,
   O'er the rocky hights and steepness,
As with misty mantle cov'ring,
   Every nook and cave-like deepness.

Here I dwell with Nymphs and Dryads;
   Here, so high perched on the mountains;
While my everlasting waters
   Flutter down in ceaseless fountains.

---

* A beautiful water-fall near " Wawona," Mariposa County, visited
by tourists on their way to Yosemite.

Out I leap into the sunshine,
　　Toss my silv'ry locks before me;
While, as kneeling on my footstool,
　　Lo! the river floods adore me.

Dashing into space so grandly,
　　Naiad streams are dancing lightly;
With a million scintillations,
　　Spangling all the air so brightly.

Or from cliff or turret springing,
　　As in steely armor's brightness,
On their foaming steeds descending,
　　Ghostly knights in robes of whiteness.

In the Sylvan grotto hiding,
　　See my bride her bright hair tosses,
Shim'ring down in glist'ning meshes,
　　'Mong the lovely ferns and mosses.

I am ruler of these forests;
　　I am noisy in my clamor,
As old Jove's resounding thunders,
　　As old Vulcan's ringing hammer.

With a thousand eyes I'm gleaming,
　　And my white beard wildly tosses,
As rude Boreas, jealous-hearted,
　　O'er my mountain passes crosses.

What care I for howling tempests,
  As I chant, in joyful singing,
Praises to the God who made me,
  Echo with my chorus ringing.

Lo! the Frost King brings his shackles,
  Ties my limbs with strength and power,
While his Elves are deftly weaving,
  Shroud, and wreath, and snowy flower.

Though he tries with deathly stillness,
  But to hush my voice forever;
I leap out from his embraces,
  And his manacles I sever.

For I'm Monarch of these forests,
  From my great throne high and lonely,
Shouting out to lesser streamlets,
  I reign o'er these waters only.

I am mighty in my power,
  I am splendid in my glory,
What care I for Neptune's oceans,
  Famed in song, and ancient story.

FORGIVE.

Forgive, forgive! yes, every wrong forgive,
  Nor with lack charity turn thou away,
From one who pardon seeks; if thou wouldst hope to live
  In Heaven's supernal glories, endless day,
        Thou must all wrongs forgive.

Though those thou dream'dst were ever faithful friends,
  Have pressed thy brow with but a traitor's kiss,
And thy forsaken heart deep anguish rends,
  Did not our Lord betrayed e'en suffer this,
        Yet patiently forgive?

Lo! from the cross Christ speaks to me, to you,
  He, the great God in man, who had all power,
Said: "Father, forgive them—they know not what they do;"
  Prayed for his slayers, in that awful hour,
        And so must we forgive.

HEART WOES.

What woe like mine? sighed a widow pale,
As she bowed her head 'neath her sable vail;
Ah! who more desolate, sad and lone,
Cries up for help to the Maker's throne?

What woe like mine? cried a weeping maid,
By a dastard's broken vow betrayed;
Oh! who will pity my stricken heart
'Mong the selfish throngs that crowd life's mart?

What woe like mine? moaned a gray-haired sire,
As he saw his only son expire;
Ah! who is left to blazon my name
On the shining scroll of immortal fame?

What woe like mine? wept a mother dear,
As she sobbing bent o'er her infant's bier;
What comfort for me on earth is left,
By death of my bosom's pride bereft?

Time passed on, and the widow pale
Blushed 'neath the folds of a bridal vail;
The maid laid her smiling face to rest
On a new love's fond and faithful breast.

The sire, his moments of life are told
In heaping his shining gods of gold;
But the mother, smitten by sorrow's wraith,
Looks up to God in trusting faith.

LINDA.

Swathed in her winding sheet she laid,
    Past Youth's ideal dreaming;
And the moonbeams through the casement strayed
And over her pallid features played,
    With white and ghastly gleaming.

Too sensitive heart so steeped in wo,
    Too frail thy life's threads blending;
Affection crushed that still would glow,
Writhing in misery's keenest throe
    Scorn—love—and life contending.

But stars will shine though clouds may hide
    Their sparkles through heaven glancing;
So love may live through wrong and pride
Still gushes and floats the reckless tide,
    Like Will o' wisp entrancing.

Yet in the flush of youth's lovliest dawn,
    When the soul looks forth unshrinking;
'Ere by the wrenchings of misery torn,
When life seems an Eden, the heart like the morn,
    But sunbeams of happiness drinking.

Linda the gentle—Linda the fair,
    The child of mirth and gladness;

Till that breast was pierced by the fangs of care,
And sorrow had nursed her vultures there,
    Goading the brain to madness.

Day came, and went, and the night drew near,
    Her phantom reign resuming;
So stormy and bleak, so vast and drear,
That the bosom quaked with spectral fear,
    Amid the wierd-like glooming.

And blighted she lay so chill and cold,
    Crushed down in youth's young blooming;
'Ere yet life's twentieth summer was told,
Death clasped her form in his icy fold,
    Faith, hope and love entombing.

And he who filled that heart with care,
    His mind yet conscience haunting;
Shall feel as fiends held orgies there,
And fiery scorpions made their lair,
    Forever wildly taunting.

So fadeless her slumber, so fixed and deep,
    So rigid, so unheeding;
Oh ! Ye might not break that stony sleep,
In vain shall the wretched mourners weep,
    In vain grief's frantic pleading.

Joy's sparkling goblet had met thy lip,
    Bright as the sunny beamings,
That into the shining waters dip,
But too oft like them the hopes we sip
    Are false and transient gleamings.

DEATH.

We are marching, ever marching,
    To the open gates of death;
We are nearing with each moment,
    With each pulse throb, and each breath;
Ever onward is life's journey,
    Never backward can we turn,
Though all rugged be the pathway.
    And the skies look dark and stern.

Some are hast'ning, madly hast'ning,
    On to meet the victor knight,
Others loiter by the wayside,
    And will shrink to face his blight;
While 'mid rev'ling scenes of pleasure,
    Crowds are gathered in the dance,
Hearts are smitten ev'ry instant
    By the ghostly monarch's lance.

All marriage bells gladly ringing
  Joy on the shining air they send,
Yet each knell brings bride and bridegroom,
  Ever nearer to time's end;
And the warrior, proudly rushing,
  'Mid the fearful battle's strife,
For his country or for glory,
  Yields to Death his mortal life.

See the maid, in love's first dreaming,
  Cast, like faded lily down;
'Mid life's sorrowing or gladness
  All must meet Death's blasting frown,
Lo, he gathers youth like roses,
  Locks whitening with time's snow,
Young manhood and the baby faces,
  By his spell are stricken low.

In the land of fair Italia,
  Or the icy, frigid zone,
Mortal captives aye are falling
  'Round the ruthless slayer's throne.
We are marching, ever marching,
  To the open gates of death,
We are nearing with each moment,
  With each pulse throb and each breath

ARE THEY ALL FALSE.

Of all the virtues that grace our earth.
  Doth friendship never act a part?
Or must gold ever form the welding link;
  To fetter a comrade's heart?
The cheerful smile on a winning face,
  Is it but deception's mask?
The kindly glance, and clasping hand,
  Are they false must we ever ask?

The gentle tone, the soothing word,
  May ye trust--may the heart believe?
When the lips that loudest would sound our praise,
  Have been the first to deceive?
The guileful speech of a flattering tongue,
  Too oft true friendship may win;
But beware--the jewels that deck the form,
  Ne'er bespeak the heart within.

Those that we meet in the festive hall,
  That share in our mirthful glee,
Will they cheer us still if misfortune comes
  With its boon of misery?
Are they false, all false the mortal throngs?
  Are there no pure friendships given?
No tie to bind true heart to heart,
  And link the soul with heaven?

I know in circle of home fond love
    In faithful candor glows;
In changeless bloom, like ever-green tree,
    Amid joy or blasting woes;
But friendship, are thy links but formed of gold
    Or self interest that firmly dwell?
Nay thy powers have bound some human hearts,
    With a deathless heaven-born spell.

THE BLOOMING SPRINGTIME COMES.

Behold the blooming springtime comes,
    Robed in flowers, and gemmed with dew,
The heavens a brilliant splendor wear,
    A deeper and a lovelier blue.
She comes so like a timid maid,
    With eyes of light and cheeks of bloom,
Oh, smile to greet her mortals all,
    Let not one heart be steeped in gloom.
Shining she comes as dazzling bright,
    As hopes to the unclouded heart.
And yet, alas! like thee, wierd hope,
    Will all her loveliness depart;
Yet blissful time thou wilt return,
    To cheer us with thy birds and flow'rs,
As sorrow like the blighting frost,
    Will pass and joy again be ours.

Thou rose-crown'd nymph, what bring'st thou now,
　Amid thy buds and leaflets green,
Must war our country desolate ?
　The heart from thy dear charms to wean ?
Shall pestilence thy zephers taint,
　And with thy glowing sunshine play?
Ah! no, let blushing health come forth,
　And strew with gladness all the way.
Whil'st thou in bride like beauty reign'st,
　Shall mortals bow in sorrow's weeds?
Great Spirit shield us from these ills,
　This heart in humble anguish pleads.
Glorious season, springtime golden.
　Queen season of the train art thou,
Thy warm kiss wakes the ice bound streams,
　And sunbeams wreath thy radiant brow.

Thy morn with songs of birds steps forth,
　Flinging across the azure skies,
Her banner so superbly blent,
　Of silvery gleams and rosy dies.
Thy fading twilight who may paint,
　When gorgeous hues all heaping rest,
Like fairy bowers by magic strewn,
　So richly in the dusky west.
Thy moonlight so serenely calm,
　So holy, ever seems to tell,
Of fairer worlds where blessed souls,

Shall in eternal springtime dwell.
I love thee, oh! thou season fair,
  A hallow'd spell from thee is cast
O'er human hearts, that lingers there,
  Like some bright presence from the past.

THE BELLE.

Rosy cheeks and beaming eyes.
  Cherry lips and forehead white;
Many a hapless lover sighs
  'Neath her glances burning bright.

Grace in every movement charms,
  Beauty from each dark tress peeps;
'Gainst her bachelor hearts in arms,
  Constant war her magic keeps.

Rings her laugh in music sweet
  As the rills mellifluous lay;
Or the notes glad birds repeat,
  As they greet the new-born day.

Seems there angels at her side,
  Bidding evil spells depart;
Pray they not no ill betide,
  Sorrow never rend her heart.

Ne'er should envy's cruel speech,
  Strive to make her heart distres't;
As the snake will slyly reach
  And sting the birdling in its nest.

This fair lady that I know,
  Liveth in a sylvan bower;
Heart pure as the sinless snow,
  Blest with all the muses pow'r.

No coquette this winsome lass,
  But nature's own bewitching child;
Fair as daisy in the grass,
  Gentle, modest, meek and mild.

Who shall win the lovely prize?
  Lucky wight indeed were he,
While on earth beneath those eyes,
  Paradise would seem to be.

VIRTUE AND VICE.

Virtue belov'd of angels and revered by men,
In features fair as are the holy throngs of God;
Beauteous and radiant with undying youth,
Ever cheering and comforting the honest heart.
While reason, and truth, with solemn and thoughtful mien,
Fearless direct and guide her on her sinless road;

The syren hope in gladdening tones e'er singing,
Leadeth on the way with standard brightly gleaming.
And ever at her side comes charity and faith,
In sweet attendance, mingling pure—mild charity
With placid countenance and kind and gentle speech,
Ever on men bestowing her good and blessed gifts;
While faith with glowing torch, and eyes and hand uplifted,
Points the repentant soul to happiness beyond.

But vice comes by, with upas breath destroying,
Decrepid with age, yet bedecked in glowing hues;
Enticing mortals o'er seeming flowery path,
Which doth but end in woe, in sorrowing and sin.
And with her shameless Malice and foul Envy came;
The one with venom'd tongue the direst evil speaking,
While envy at others' rights did base, and vainly grasp;
And in her train gay folly tript, a mindless maid,
Startling the air with her most boisterous laugh;
Aye, treacherously leading blindfold conscience on,
'Till she looks forth too late to find herself misled.
Throughout all space they pass'd, but few to Virtue bow'd.
While yet to Vice her myriad votaries clung.

Two beings were, one followed and sought after Vice,
And hapless lived a life of bitterness and strife.
And died in woful wretchedness—none cared his fate,
None wept his loss nor ever kept his mem'ry dear.
The other Virtue loved, and ever cheerful lived

2

In sweet content, and when the dark winged angel came,
Pass'd out mourned and lamented by the world at large;
For Virtue all admired, though few her precepts kept,
And still chose Vice in her deceptive mood,
To the lovelier radiance of her chaster mien.

Lo! in a narrow way, led by the star of faith,
Behold true woman, stepping to this side then to that
To counsel straying hearts—smoothing the sick one's couch,
Giving to hungry need, sweet comfort whispering
To departing souls; hiding from a mocking world
The faults of others. No twinge of envy stirs her heart,
Rejoiced by others' weal. Lo! Malice in vain
Like serpent stings at her, with poison'd fang,
She keeps the path that Virtue points—giving sweet words
For slander's burning darts—raising her fallen foe.
To frosted age she tender reverence pays;
Ever in her soul the assembled Virtues dwell,
Strewing life's ways with blessings kind, as Summer fair
Scattered o'er earth her precious fruits and flowers.

But woman, led by vanity and envy dire.
Flung 'neath the gilded car of Vice her once pure heart,
'Till all the Virtues there were crushed or trampled out;
And in their place malice and slander sat enthroned,
And she did jibe and jeer at perfect womanhood,
And put within their way great stumbling blocks to wound,
Rude, sneering taunts to mock and turn their steps aside,

Holding their goodness forth a scorn unto her mates,
Scoffing that they should wed for love, nor sell themselves,
For gold, and stand before the world a living lie;
With face of smiles cov'ring a rotten traitor heart.
Like stainless sepulchre rear'd o'er corruption's work,
'Till sinking, step by step, from vice to vice, they plunge,
Dragging once spotless souls down to pollution's dens.
Thou beauteous earth, why art thou so debased and fallen?
Nor still perfect as first from the Creator's hand ?
Immortal souls why are ye so to evil prone ?
If good ye love, why in iniquity so defiled ?
Oh! flee from Vice, from baneful inclinations turn,
And let Virtue be helmsman in the voyage of life.

SUNSHINE.

Beauteous Sunshine, gorgeous Sunshine,
How I love its molten beams;
Pressing now against my casement,
Like bright fantasies in dreams.
Bringing back life's ways of glory,
Childhood with its gleesome days;
Blissful time, whose griefless joying,
Made the heart one sunny blaze.

When the merry Christmas brought us,
    Mirth and gladness with the hours,
'Ere the heart had learned life's realness,
    How hopes wither like the flow'rs;
Fade, and banish like the sunbeams,
    With which in childish sport we played;
Grasping at their gleamy network,
    That against the wall was laid.

Oh! the Sunshine, Nature's Poet,
    Fingers dipt in heav'nly light;
That on every leaf, and flower,
    God's sweet poesy doth write.
Flooding all the mid-day zenith,
    With wavy seas of amber tinge;
Circling western skies at even,
    With shining threads of golden fringe.

Slanting through the open doorway.
    Quiv'ring column's gleaming bright;
Seeming like daguerred reflections.
    From the home of endless light.
In my heart paints scene of rapture,
    Sweet Contentment's picture fair;
Faithful love beside the hearth-stone,
    Sits like watching angel there.

O'er Chowchilla's hills and chasms,
    Apollo darting beamings launches;

Shim'ring on the Merced's waters,
  Gold rain sifting through the branches;
Flaming up like grand Vesuvius,
  Brazen shafts so high, and spiry;
Glist'ning on the steeples summit,
  Burning rays so wierd and fiery.

On Yosemite's high mountains,
  Dripping with an arid glare;
Sparkling on their snow-wreath'd foreheads,
  Like glist'ning diamonds cluster'd there;
Nestling in that mystic valley.
  Peeping in the sylvan dell;
All the herd and sportive lambkins,
  Wreathing with a cheery spell.

Sunny gleams on baby faces,
  Glow there like the smile of God;
As still unto his arms he hailed them,
  When, as man, our earth he trod;
And in mercy to Nain's widow,
  Bowed 'neath Sorrow's dark control;
Bade her son fling off Death's shackles,
  And life's sunshine light his soul.

Oh! the Sunshine, blessed Sunshine,
  Semblance of the love divine;
Which, though clouds awhile obscure them,
  Through their gloom stray beamings shine:

So Heaven's ever watchful spirit,
   'Mid life's trials, 'mid its woes;
Whispers of a sinless Eden,
   Where eternal Sunshine glows.

A WHISPER TO ALL.

Ah! Mortals, let us fondly cherish,
   All affections that are ours;
For by negligence they perish,
   As unnoticed prairie flowers,
When no zephyr comes and fanneth,
   Their frail leaflets parch'd and heated,
So the heart's affection waneth,
   If by kindest love not greeted.

If fond hands with deeds of kindness,
   All life's ways with peace are strewing
Turn not thou in thoughtless blindness,
   To the untried's tender wooing;
Words alone oh! ne'er are showing,
   How true a heart may be to thee,
But kindly acts from fond souls flowing,
   Breathe forth their pure sincerity.

Actions speak the heart's devotion,
  Every deed a something telling;
As many rivers form the ocean,
  Every drop the current swelling,
If harsh words come thy soul surprising
  Starts thy breast to angers burning;
Turn not thou in fierce despising,
  From confiding love's true yearning.

Not for foibles doubt the trusted,
  Doubt not those long years were proving
Not by thee the lance be thrusted,
  Severing the ties so loving;
Rather prove them false and changing,
  Whom ye dream't not could deceive;
Than in wayward quick estranging,
  Bid a faithful bosom grieve.

Mortal, if thou art perfection,
  Then all wisely seek another;
Seeming but thine own reflection,
  By thy merits judge thy brother,
Or prize affections now that bless thee,
  Dream they are kindly gifts from heaven,
While the folding arms caress thee,
  For God may take back that He's given.

AN ELEGY.

There's a jubilee in Heaven,
    And the pearl gates stand ajar:
And the Seraph throngs are shouting,
    From that shining world afar:
" Come up, ye beauteous Spirits,
    From your pain and sickness come;
Lovely Sister—gentle Brother—
    Welcome to our blissful home!"

Though Death reaps a precious harvest,
    Mowing youth and beauty down,
At Heav'n's gate the angels wait them
    With the blest immortal crown;
But tears fall in burning torrents,
    And each heart in anguish grieves,
As we see the dear ones lying
    Like the blasted Autumn leaves.

Oh! Death reaps a precious harvest;
    See his sickle's sharpen'd side
Smites the kind, devoted daughter—
    The sorrowing mother's pride.
Weeping mother, mourning sister,
    In your love so wildly fond,
Know you not your household Angel
    Shineth in the courts beyond?

See! the youth, in budding manhood,
  Lieth stricken, pale and low;
Closed the kind eyes' gladsome beaming,
  Cold the high and manly brow.
But the same great God that tempers
  The rude winds to the shorn lamb,
Sends faith, lone, sorrowing brother,
  Your anguished woe to calm.

How we miss *his* kindly greeting!
  How we miss *her* heav'nly smile!
Why, oh! Death, the fond heart cheating?
  Why with treach'rous hopes beguile?
Send Thy spirit, blessed Saviour,
  To each hopeless mourner's breast,
Tell them of that bright Hereafter,
  Where there lost and loved ones rest.

Look up! look up! Ye lone weepers,
  With true faith in your distress;
List! a still small voice is whisp'ring,
  "I'll not leave ye comfortless!"
Then prepare to meet your dear ones
  On that bright but distant shore;
There, in joy, they wait your coming,
  Where you'll meet to part no more.

Rosy Blossoms! in life's Springtime
  Blasted by Death's sudden Frost;

Shining meteors! gleaming jewels!
  In Time's mighty ocean lost!
There's a jubilee in Heaven,
  In our midst grief's tempest rolls;
But there's jubilee in Heaven—
  Seraphs hail two ransomed Souls !

SUMMER TIME. .

All hail! oh, all hail! to the Summer time,
Let's greet her now in her glorious prime;
With a pean of joy a pean of mirth,
While her smile still gladdens the blooming earth,
While verdure is decking valley and field,
And Nature her offering of beauty may yield;
While her bright smile lingers on hill and glade.
Ere the blossom shall fall or leaflet fade.

Come away—away from the cheerless strife,
The tedious course of a city life;
Oh! come where the song of the gleesome bird,
In the green wildwood is joyously heard;
Where the rill down the mountain gaily leaps,
And violet in quiet languor sleeps;
Yes, come to the dingle, come to the dell,
Where Summer is wreathing her richest spell.

Come! come while the tiniest insect's voice,
Seems to bid every human heart rejoice;
For now may ye worship at Nature's shrine,
Where the flowers in rich luxuriance twine,
As wreathed by magic of fairy fingers,
Haste while the spirit of beauty lingers;
Ah! come ere the demon of dark decay,
Shall sweep the gems from our path away.

View yon cottage home on the meadow green;
There never sounds voice of sorrow, I ween;
There childhood is sporting in mirthful glee,
With no cankering thought of misery;
Aye, greeted at morn with a mother's blessing,
At eve with a father's kind caressing;
There Summer her treasured gifts doth bestow,
And the heart ne'er harbors the sigh of woe.

But change the scene.   Lo! the wintry blast,
With shriek and moan, goes hurrying past
A city home, by the once glad hearth;
Lo! sorrow stifles the song of mirth.
There Poverty gathers her raiment scant;
There wails forth the piteous cry of want
From Infancy's lips—while the wind sweeps by,
O'erladen with moanings of agony.

Let us greet, O, Summer! thy radiant bloom,
Ere Autumn shall come with his death-like gloom;

For thou speak'st to the heart of hope and joy,
No thought of sorrow would e'er annoy;
Ere we had dreamed that the kindliest smile
Oft marked but deception's mask the while;
Ere reality's fearful lessons were taught,
And we lived in a dreamy world of thought.

I love, how I love thy glittering blaze—
It speaks to my heart of my childhood's days;
Of the home where my early footsteps wandered,
Where first in sweet fancy's realm I pondered;
Back, oh! rolls back each buried year,
With its doubts, and its hopes, its joy and fear,
An offering, oh! sad as withered flowers,
Lo! memory brings forth its faded hours.

When twilight her gorgeous banner hath unfurled,
And night spreads her star-gemmed wings o'er the world,
Ah! then how my fond heart clings to thee!
For thou breathest of a fairer world to me;
How I love—yes, I love thy sunny beams,
When the waters sport with myriad gleams;
When Nature with hymning of triumph rings,
As morn from her rosy cavern springs,
Scattering the dew from her glowing wings.

Yes, there's balm, there's joy in each glistening ray,
Too fleeting thy course, too hurried thy stay;
Too soon must we mourn o'er thy dazzling flight,

When thy bright leaves droop, 'neath the Autumn's blight;
Too soon must the frost-Monarch claim thy throne;
Too soon is thy fragile splendor flown;
But I hail, and bless thy glorious reign,
For I ne'er might look on thy charms again.

<hr>

FOREBODING.

Why forever foreboding of griefs ere they dawn,
" Enough for to-day is the evil that's born,"
O why, while the heart may be free from all sorrow,
Cloud the peace of to-day with dread of to-morrow?
For why should the trials we've met in the past,
A gloom o'er our present unceasingly cast?
'Tis time for thy dreading when care shall beset,
Nor shadow life's sunshine with woes that we've met.
Why ever suspecting that terrors are near?
Why list for the tempest ere storm clouds appear?
While the morning is beaming, why picture the night?
When the rose is in bloom why dream of its blight?
Why dread for thine infant a pathway of sin?
Nor list to hope's whisperings of glories he'll win?
Why trace 'neath the bloom of the bride's snowy wreath
The dark ghoul of woes, or phantom of death?
The lights of the future ne'er dim with a tear,

But with faith, and with hope, meet the ills that are here.
When dear friends are round thee, why thinking the while
Of sadness and partings—rather seek to beguile
The sorrow of others, the spectre of care,
Cast out from thy bosom.   Beware, oh! beware!
Nor thus waste life's years, for soon the last toll
Of time for thee here shall resound on thy soul.

------◆------

TIME OF FLOWERS.

Thou'rt gone, thou'rt gone, glad time of flowers,
   Lost, lost in eternity;
Leaving of sad, and of blissful hours,
   A chequered memory
      Of griefs and joys.

Thou'rt gone in thy pomp, and splendor by,
   Like visions of love and truth;
Thy leaves all withered and lifeless lie,
   As the treasured hopes of youth
      Which time destroys.

Thou'rt gone, as gleams of the golden day,
   May fade 'mid the storm and cloud,
As Peace may flee from the earthly way,
   And fearful sorrows enshroud
      The yearning soul.

Though Joy hath gladdened the heart awhile,
　Grief may dim the future years,
O'er faces that beam'd with a cheerful smile,
　Now the heart wrung bitter tears
　　　　May hopeless flow.

Thou'rt gone, but with thee too hath fled,
-　Full many a joyous dream,
Fleeting and frail as the rich beams shed
　By sunlight, on the stream,
　　　　So dazzling bright.

Thou'rt gone as the spell of Innocence
　May flee from the human heart;
'Tis sad, Oh! earth that so oft from thence,
　Truth's holiest gems depart
　　　　Like fading light.

Thou'rt gone, and Love once fondly cherished
　Where the heart with faith relied,
Like the rainbow hues hath changed or perished,
　They ye dreamt years had tried,
　　　　The trusted friend.

Yet through all, ah, let my heart still dwell,
　In its own bright world of thought;
Let not the falseness of life dispel,
　The visions by fancy wrought,
　　　　Let nought e'er rend.

But still let affection's cheerful ray,
  Like beams from the throne above,
Light for aye all my earthly way,
  With a dream of changeless Love—
    A deathless tie.

Oh! still let the bride in trusting Hope,
  Smile on the love-crowned hours;
And her future moments in sunshine ope,
  On a world of fadeless flowers,
    And cloudless sky.

Thou'rt gone, thou'rt gone, and many that hailed
  With joy thy radiant birth;
'Mid the bloom the roseate cheek hath paled,
  And withered away from earth,
    Yet evermore.

To greet thy smile in that shining sphere,
  Beyond the immortal skies,
Where the soul shall meet all it e'er loved here,
  Where Truth—Beauty never dies—
    The blessed shore.

A SONG FOR THE TIMES.

List ! and I'll sing you a song of the times,
Of dollars and cents and dollars and dimes,
Of the kindly greeting of friendly hands,
That value you for your houses and lands,
That will feast with you in your hours of joy,
Yet never are near when sorrows annoy.
But mark, if your fortunes are going down,
Hands cease to clasp and a snub or a frown
Is all you will meet in our modern times,
Of dollars and cents and dollars and dimes.

Like Israel's tribe in the wilderness,
Now the "Golden Calf" is the God some bless.
Why for the paltry dollar man sells his soul ?
Jingle of twenties the musical role
That leads a mother to sell for a price
Her child for a wife, for it is so nice
To know she is rich.   Ah ! better a nun,
Than marry a man who never has won
The fresh young heart—even the love for Christ,
In our modern times is bartered and priced.

My lady from gold and silver can dine,
Can ride in her carriage on cushions fine,
Youth and her beauty, all eagerly sold,
To a man who's wrinkled, ugly and old,

All for rich jewels and splendor in dress,
She's wed to a life of much wretchedness,
All for a mansion and a high estate,
She has tied herself to a bitter fate.
Yes, wives are thus bought in our modern times,
For dollars and cents and dollars and dimes.

At your well spread board comes a smiling face,
That in bankrupt home leaves a vacant place,
Where the butterfly friend has fled from sight,
As they felt the doom of misfortunes blight,
Ever on hand with a word of advice,
As they grasp your purse with the strength of a vice,
For loan a peep in your pocket they take,
As fishing for coin for a banking stake,
But would scout your name for the worst of crimes,
If you chance to lose your dollars and dimes.

Oh ! come back ye days of old forty-nine,
With the canvas pants, and the dripping mine,
Where judge, and lawyer, friendly met
With brave mechanics, where each brow was wet
With honest toil, and each loved as his life,
The little missives from children and wife,
And woman was honored among their fold,
More precious by far than their well-earned gold,
An idol to worship—but in these times,
They adore a man for his dollars and dimes.

Oh ! I turn in shame from our modern ways,
Give me the kind hearts of the good old days,
When a miner's shirt hid manlier breast,
Than now is enrobed in a silken vest,
When man was a man, though he dug the sod,
And the foot of wealth was not basely trod
On earth's lowliest ones—but help in need
Was motto of all, when the gospel creed
Taught their duty to each, but now the plan
Is to filch the pockets of fellow man.

Yes, to filch his pockets and turn him loose,
When his cash gives out.   Oh! men have no use
For those they have wronged, no grateful need
To offer you back for a kindly deed,
In the times when your coin was gladly lent,
To those who knew not what gratitude meant,
Though you their fortunes in life may now carve,
They might leave your wife and children to starve,
The heart grows earth-sick amid these times,
When one is loved for his dollars and dimes.

Even they of your childhood's household band,
Will forget to clasp with a faithful hand,
If your cash gives out you've seldom a friend,
Though you travel the land from end to end,
My soul turns away from earth's glitter and glare,
To those who have climbed up the golden stair,

Whose dear forms now lie alone in the dust,
Whose friendship was true, in whom we could trust,
For whose footsteps we list'n in mem'rys halls,
Dearest of faces that hang on her walls.

-----◆-- --

IN GRIEF'S STORM CLOUD.

In grief's storm cloud there's a rifting,
Where the light of heaven is drifting,
And supernal glories sifting,
    Into the dreary breast.

When we feel as drawing nearer
To Christ's love, when growing dearer,
And faith's visions brighten clearer,
    As now, with Him, we rest.

All the air with gladness thrilling,
As a wild bird's gleesome trilling,
My fond soul with rapture filling,
    Till earth an Eden glows.

Cease, ah! cease your sad foreboding,
The lorn spirit ever goading,
And the heart forever loading
    With fears of coming woes.

See, the pearly gates unfolden,
And faith points to mansions, olden,
Where the shining streets are golden
    In the city of the blest.

Let thy heart, earth's trials scorning,
With the bright stars of the morning
Ever praise the lovely dawning
    Of God's eternal rest.

Though the ones we prized so dearly,
And whose friendship shown so clearly;
We never dreamt 'twas merely
    The motto, all for self.

Till the time had come for trials,
And we drank from fiery vials,
But to find as false Belials,
    They loved us for our pelf.

And a presence seems to move me
Into looking up above me,
Where those hearts who truly love me
    At heaven's portals wait.

Though earth were filled with sorrow,
And there seldom dawns a morrow,
That does not seem to borrow
    A warning of sad fate.

Of the footsteps worn and weary,
That once plod in pathways dreary,
Without one bright hope that's cheery
    To gild the way of life.

Neath earth's burdens ever bending,
O'er care's thorny brambles wending,
Ever longing for the endiug
    Of bitterness and strife.

Though with bleeding feet aye treading,
Where no rose breaths sweet are shedding,
And the smile of God is spreading
    A glory as ye wend.

Then look up from grief's distressing,
To that day of heavenly blessing,
Of a Saviour's kind caressing
    When time and earth shall end.

YOSEMITE.

The gates unbarred and the sword withheld,
Yosemite, as that Eden of eld,
    Enchants the pilgrim's view;
Like that lovely garden, glad home of Eve,
E'er Satan lured her to deceive,
    From paths of virtue true.

And through its midst in Naiad song,
The shimmering waters carol along,
    Gracefully sweep and glide;
While all the meadows the wild flowers strew,
Like coral beds of every hue;
    That ocean caverns hide.

Out in the sunshine gauzily rolled,
With rainbows braiding each spangled folds,
    The Bridal Veil drips her rain;
While like mammoth monster in earthquake shocks,
Yosemite leaps o'er the sullen rocks,
    Shaking his foamy mane.

Lo, the Virgn's tears as bright crystals gleam,
And pour in a mournful, quivering stream,
    As if in endless woe;
Eve still wept the hour the Archangel came,
And from their bowers in grief and shame,
    Bade our first parents go.

See Mirror Lake, as so mystical there,
The seraphs penciled the landscape fair,
    With Morn's rosy-finger tipt,
Daguerreotyped on its waters lie,
Trees, mounts, and rocks and heaven's blue sky,
    Grottoes and caverns crypt.

Lo, the Vernal fall glides as sea nymphs lost,
That o'er the mountain are giddily tost,
        Shim'ring with gleaming pearls;
And spanning their edge in shining bands,
Seemeth netted jewels in lacy strands
        As it quaintly curves and curls.

Nevada's waters like a shattered cloud,
Or a drift of snowflakes, the dark rocks shroud
        And fall in diamond showers;
As if ghostly elves from the summit leap
And lie in a glistening, glassy heap
        Of bright immortal flowers.

On Cloud's Rest a splendid glory is lain,
As sunset spatters a golden rain,
        In a mesh of colors bright;
As if Heaven's portals had opened wide,
And the mountain height had glorified,
        With a glow of celestial light.

In leafy grottoes and mystical grove,
The sunbeams in a gleamy net-work wove,
        Their shining banners trail;
Where turrets, and minarets, and tower,
So grandly reared, proclaim His power,
        Who built this lovely vale?

From the world's false glitter, fain would I come,
And nestle in thee, thou Paradise home.
    Surely God meets us here;
Where marvelous nature each sense appalls,
As cathedral domes and as castle walls,
    His wondrous works appear.

DOTH THY FACE SPEAK THY HEART?

By joyous laugh—and bright eyes glance,
    Seldom the inward soul ye tell;
It may be pierced by sorrow's lance,
Though awhile it rests in seeming trance,
    Oh! nought may mem'ry's pow'r dispel:
        The thoughtful mirror wherein ye see,
        The past—with its joy or misery.

'Twere right if e'er the smiling face,
    Would speak a glad and griefless breast,
Couldst look within there ye may trace
Sorrow hath found a nestling place,
    Filling the heart with strange unrest,
        Wrapping in mildew's withering blight,
        Where gleam'd, we dreamt, joy's sunny light.

Ah! ne'er should woes lie hidden deep,
  Within the inmost bosom's cell,
O'er which the secret heart will weep,
And many a dreary vigil keep,
  Weaving a strange, unearthly spell.
    Griefs that some treasur'd hope hath slain,
    That may not spring to life again.

Falsehood, thou direst wo to feel,
  When those we dreamt so true and kind,
Try the soul on an Ixion wheel,
'Till the bewilder'd brain will reel!
  Like whirlwind the astonish'd mind ;
    But some there are—can bear with all,
    'Fore which the feebler natures fall.

A hapless maiden pines in vain,
  O'er perjured lover's broken vow,
The spell her very soul doth chain,
Life seems a siege of endless pain,
  And false the smiles that wreathe her brow,
    She wastes on mortal that firm love,
    She should have placed on God above

Ambition, too, will moaning sigh,
  O'er dying hopes by fancy nurst,
Fame's towers, in vision built so high,
That now in scattered ruins lie,

As bubbles in the sunlight burst!
  Yet smiles upon his face we greet,
  That may the keenest searcher cheat.

But oh! 'tis wrong God's gift to slight,
  Of life—to pine o'er mortal wo,
Why turn its sunshine into night?
Why sear thy youth with useless blight?
  For all Faith's stars do quenchless glow,
    If ye but trust our truest friend,
    Nor aye on self too much depend.

Love not this world too wildly well,
  But seek with thankfulness of heart,
All brooding discontent to quell,
Cast from thy soul its evil spell,
  The griefs long dead to life may start;
    Oh! fling them back and still bear on,
    Think all thy blessed Savior's borne.

JESSIE FAUSE LOVE.

Young Jessie was a bashfu' lass,
  Wi' locks o' chestnut hue,
Wi' dimplin' chin and bloomin' cheek,
  An' e'en o' bonnie blue.

Sae sweetly
An' neatly
She deck'd her wi' sic care,
Sae tastily
An' chastely,
Her ev'ry look an air.

Her tiny feet cam' peepin' out
Frae 'neath her gown o' snaw,
Like elfies dartin' on your sight,
Sae wee and unco' sma'
Her shinin, teeth,
Like pearly wreath,
Glint frae her rosy mou'
Could you but see,
You'd own wi' me
Nae cantier lass ye knew.

Her rounded throat and slender waist,
Nae bonnier e'er ye dream'd,
Her forehead a' sae white an' high,
O' sculptur'd marble seem'd.
Sae blandly
An' grandly
Her archin' brows were laid.
Her glancin',
Entrancin',
Her mirthfu' heart betray'd.

Beside the waefu' couch o' pain,
  Or where lane anguish pin'd,
Wi' soothin' word, an' ruefu' mien
  The faithfu' lass you'd find.
        Sae tearfu'
        An' fearfu'
To see anither smart,
        An' bearin'
        An' sharin'
Their waes wi' a' her heart.

Wi' winnin' speech an' guilefu' tongue,
  Wi' a' wizard's art,
A fause chield cam wi' flatt'rin' words,
  An' won puir Jessie's heart.
        Deceivin'
        An' leavin'
Her sorrowfu' to pine.
        Sae palely
        An' frailly
She drooped like a vine.

Tho' sair her heart she strave to bear
  The wrang her saul had met;
Yet tears frae out her dowie e'en,
  Fu' aft her cheeks had wet.
        Sae faintly
        An' saintly

Her smile sae mournfu' shone,
  Alake! alake!
  Her heart maist break,
Her peace o' mind had flown.

An' tho', like simmer's clouded sky,
  Her way gat fu' o' gloom,
Yet weel she kenn'd 'twas fearfu' sin
  To greet aboon her doom;
      An' mild-like
      An' child-like
She looket ay above,
      In weakness
      Wi' meekness
Still trustin' in God's love.

BE GLAD.

Be glad, be gay, in life's golden hours,
  While hope flushes the cheek and lights the eye;
For as chill wind's kiss will blight the flow'rs,
  As he floats on his with'ring mission by.

So grief will parch the rejoicing heart,
  And pale the cheek and smother the laugh,
And the soul will writhe 'neath her taunting smart,
  Till the dregs of mis'ry's chalice ye quaff.

Though riches are thine, with friendly glance,
   Tho' honor's laurels are wreathing thy fame,
Misfortune may come with her poison'd lance.
   And the friend will forget to breath thy name.

And death may circle the cherish'd form,
   And stifle the voice thou hast loved to hear,
Though hope build her pile like a beacon fire,
   Sorrow'll quench the flame with her frosty tear.

Though thy soul be cheer'd by a blissful dream,
   When heart meets heart, like the beam and spray,
Yet clouds may shadow the brightest stream,
   And darken the light of the fairest day.

Tis a weary gift, the peaceless life.
   When care ruffles the calm of the youthful breast,
Like winds and waves in boisterous strife,
   When the waters are toss'd in mad unrest.

The mother may gaze on her infant's brow,
   With visions of glory he yet might win;
But change may dim their radiant glow,
   And that life be traced in the path of sin.

Though many may greet with kindly smile,
   And the hours flit by in unsullied bliss,
Yet lips thou hast deem'd so free from guile,
   May but press thy brow with a Judas kiss.

Then be glad, be joyful while youth is there,
  While the heart speaks forth from the happy face;
Ere in the folds of the glossy hair,
  The footprints of speeding time ye trace.

Though Summer may come with flowery bloom,
  With her soft'ning skies and genial showers,
Yet Winter will follow with torpid gloom,
  As the dim night steals on the daylight hours.

Then be glad, be gleesome while yet ye may,
  While ye gather around the social hearth;
Tho' life has many a sunny way,
  Sorrow and sadness are types of earth.

———→•←———

THE REAPER ANGEL.

A thousand years in the sight of God,
  Is but one day in the sight of men,
They who treadmill of sorrow have trod,
  Shall shine in garments of whiteness when
The great Arch Angel shall sound the chime,
  That heralds to all the end of time.

The end of time and the end of woe,
When the tired hands shall folding rest,

And the lame shall walk--the blind shall know
  Blessings of sight—millennium blest,
When wrong shall not triumph over right,
  When blossoms shall bloom where now there's blight.

See the rolling grains as banners sway,
  While round them the pearly seedling weaves,
As seeming to wait the reaping day,
  When harvesters gather ripening sheaves;
And so shall the longing soul await
  The Reaper Angel at heaven's gate.

HOPE.

From the Hades depths of sadness,
  Up with shout of joy I spring.
To the sunny mount of gladness,
  Soaring forth on lightsome wing.

Though the sharpen'd blade of malice
  Plunges to thy tortur'd breast,
Though the dregs of misery's chalice
  To thy quivering lips are prest,

Though of grief a sad partaker,
  He who rules the stormy deeps,
King of Kings, our God, the Maker,
  Of the tiniest thing that creeps,

Will not leave his creatures trusting,
　To grope on in sorrow's night,
Mid the taunt of envy's thrusting,
　Or mid slander's poisoned blight.

Lone and friendless ever wand'ring,
　Blindly left in sorrow's shade,
Cheerless, hopeless, sadly pond'ring,
　On the promises Christ made.

Nay from out grief's deepest glooming,
　He will lift thy soul from blight,
As His spirit burst earth's tombing,
　And soared up to worlds of light.

So the heart with gladness filling,
　By His love shall cheerful reign,
The Christian's hope in pow'r fulfilling
　As victor over grief and pain.

TOO LATE.

I fear, alas, you will come too late,
　To ask the pardon your heart must crave,
Ere her soul starts out through the door of fate,
　Ere the sad face lies in the voiceless grave;

Ah, speak at once why you turned away,
    With a stony gaze, a chilly stare,
From the one your lips was wont to praise,
    Whose fate in life you were proud to share.

Yes, he knoweth best, who knows us all,
    Why you have stept on the love so tried.
Yet o'er the mem'ry but throw a pall,
    And think of the past as one that's died,
Of one that's dead, and the coffin lid
    Has shut forever above the face,
Where ev'ry feature for aye is hid.
    As leaving to thee no mortal trace,

Down in oblivion's waters deep.
    Let's drop the coffin'd sorrow to rest,
And pray that angels may never reap,
    When God's harvest comes, the thing unblest;
Sorrow that lies there of hearts at war,
    Who'd loved for many a happy year,
Till phantom came at the open door,
    The mother of Sin with cunning leer,

With a panther's step, and tiger's stealth,
    And whispered into your guileless ear,
And led you to feel love's priceless wealth,
    Was nought in value—the oily tongue.
Of sin leading you out in the world,
    Where vice and folly around you cling;

And your dazed brain has giddily whirled.
  To sip sweets of temptation's din,

Where your manhood stoop'd low in the dust,
  So meshes of flatt'rs rop'd you in,
And blurr'd your soul with sin's cank'ring rust,
  Yes, blurred a soul she had dream'd was white;
As snowy marble, as crystal clear,
  Where no wrong to her had laid its blight,
For many a trusting, loving year.
  Yes, down in oblivion's wat'ry grave

As some clay cold corpse, let it sink and reel,
But now ask the pardon your heart must crave,
  Ere at feet of Christ thy soul shall kneel,
In its sin robed garments from earth gone out,
  Drifting afar in eternity's space,
Shuddering with fear, battling with doubt,
  Dreading to look in that Savior's face.

———•———

THE FISHERMEN.

The fishermen group on the pebbly beach,
Where the breakers like pearly fingers reach,
    And lazily slide away.
As the backing waters steadily ebb,
They spread their nets as a lacey web,
    In the rosy light of day.

And standing there in an even line,
Pulling the needle and drawing the twine,
    A spidery mesh they net,
And their mingling voices in chorus rings,
As each steadily works and gaily sings,
    With never a care or fret.

Ah, Yo! O! Ah! Yo! and Yo heave O!
And launching our boats we cheerily row,
    Far out o'er the waters deep.
Where finny mackerel and scaly shad,
In our well wrought nets are easily had,
    Though they toss, tumble and leap.

Though they flout, and flutter, and quiver, and strain,
In their briny home, oh, never again,
    Will they briskly dart and glide.
With their snow white breasts they gaily float,
As with finny sails like mermaid boat,
    They skim along with the tide.

Oh! away we dash o'er the seething foam,
Away from our mothers, our wife and home,
    Cheer of our little one's play.
And our sharp keels leave no lingering track,
Of fishermen's boats that never come back,
    Rowed to eternity's bay.

But with stormy tempest and windy wift,
Some hapless form may yet hurriedly drift
    And dash on the pebbly sand,
Away from the dear ones that love us best,
In a friendless grave among strangers to rest,
    But safe in the better land.

The sea shells lie 'long the glist'ning shore,
Echoing forever with ocean's roar,
    Or sounding as distant bells,
As if the sea nymphs there, their harps had lost,
On the beach by hurrying breakers tost,
    Ringing like funeral knells.

THE WIFE'S WELCOME.

Come to me love ere the daisy and buttercup,
    Fair on the meadow a rich carpeting spreads,
Come ere the ring-dove in love notes complaineth,
    Ere violets peep from their soft, grassy beds.
Come as the red sun sinks low in the heavens,
    And eve with her mantle our trysting place covers,
While the air is o'er burthened with oder of flowers,
    And oriole singeth its tribute to lovers.

For sure you've been true through the years that have
    tried you,
  A husband—yet lover—for aye and for aye.
E'en as Aurora when waking at dawning,
  Is met by Apollo to brighten her way,
Even so thy love hath been light to my pathway,
  Aye cheering its moments as sunshine the day.
All through the clouding and tempests of sorrow,
  It has shone on my life as a heav'n-sent ray.

Ah, come when the summer's fair lilies and roses
  Are flinging their censers of sweets on the air,
While meadow lark low in the soft grass reposes,
  Ere the corn hangeth out her bright yellow hair.
Come while the fuchsias hang gorgeous with blossoms,
  And seem as bright humming birds nestling in sleep,
While mignonettes breath is scenting the twilight,
  And blossoming myrtles o'er garden walls creep.

Come while the bee sippeth sweets from the clover,
  Ere the bare armed oaks stand as skeletons grim,
And the morn's early frosts like diamonds are glist'ning,
  And dainty quails low in the dry grasses skim.
Oh come while all life is o'erflowing with sweetness,
  In the fair month of May or blossoming June,
While earth seems an Eden in all its completeness,
  And heart and all nature alike are in tune.

HOME-FACES.

Oh! how I love the dear home-faces,
  That shone above my childish day;
Though time, with swift and hurried paces
  May bear me from their light away.
Though some for new love fly the olden,
  Too fondly trusting the untried—
The old, that gleamed like sunshine golden,
  And should have been most deified.

I can't forget the deeds of kindness
  That through life has eased my part;
I might have groped in hapless blindness
  For a true and faithful heart.
I cannot turn from tried affections,
  That have served through many a year—
That have lit with bright reflections
  All my weary pathway here.

How I love them without measure,
  And dread our lives to drift apart;
Though God has blest me with that treasure—
  A tried and faithful human heart;
But though other love enfold me,
  Of husband and of children fond,
Still, those dear, kind faces hold me
  With a mighty, heaven-wrought bond.

Still they shine, in rainbow glory,
  Pictures in sad Memory's bowers,
Like some well remembered story,
  That we've conned in by-gone hours.
And if fate our lives must sever,
  My fond soul will look back still—
To gaze on those dear faces ever,
  That ghost-like stand at Memory's sill.

CHEER EARTH'S SAD HEARTS.

Cheer earth's sad hearts nor hopelessly despond,
  Though sorrow's cup your quivering lips have drained
Faith's balm can heal the saddest torturing wound
  That e'er a fainting mortal soul hath pained.
Though false the look that once could so entrance,
  Though false the words that once could so beguile,
The light of truth beams from our Saviour's glance,
  And pure affection crowns his tender smile.

Though envy's serpent tongue would blast thy fame,
  Though whispering malice would fond hearts divide,
At last defamers shall bow low in shame,
  And plead the rocks their guilty souls to hide.
Though thou hast seen the loved by death struck down,
  And standest alone within this weary world;

The sun must shine, though clouds awhile may frown,
   So yet for thee joy's bow may be unfurled.

Though stitch, by stitch, thy food is earned each day,
   And hungry babes may cry to thee for bread,
Oh, pray, and God will ope a brighter way.
   "Ask, and it shall be given," Emanuel said.
'Tis best, like Lazarus to have suffered much,
   Nor like Dives be reckless of your soul ;
Christ still can heal, as they who once could touch
   His garment's hem, found all their plagues made whole.

Though pale disease is sapping health and life,
   And melancholy seems thy constant guest,
Let these words cheer, 'mid sickness' racking strife:
   Jehovah chasteneth those he loveth best,
Yes, meekly bow to every earthly blight,
   Though thy brow wears the thorny crown of care,
Let faith sustain 'mid pain or sorrow's night;
   Aye, look above—eternal joy is there.

Oh! blessed Lord, without thy helping hand,
   How could some meet their woes, the traitor's sting,
But 'mid all trials hopes of that "better land,"
   Help the bruised heart unto Thy cross to cling.
Shall not the souls that seek the narrow way,
   And patient strive to do a Christian part,
Look on Thy face amid that endless day,
   Thy holy promise to the pure in heart.

Then cheer sad hearts nor sorrowing repine;
  With faith's pure shield march on through all your cares;
Though now the thorny wreath your temples twine,
  He wins heaven's crown who most earth's burthen bears.
Though poverty may be your hopeless fates,
  Though want shall tear the threads of life apart,
Seraphs for each shall ope the shining gates,
  And Jesus fold you to his sinless heart.

JULY DREAMINGS—A CALIFORNIA IDYL.

Oh! Summer, fling your richest beams
  Where Flora gorgeous carpet layeth!
For my poor heart is filled with dreams,
  As back in thought's bright realm it strayeth.

Sick of the tedious commonplace,
  Of household cares that have no ending;
So, Fancy, let us have a race
  Through thy gay paths so gladly wending.

Tune your sweet castanets, ye rills,
  While ripple with the sunbeam dances;
Wake violets and daffodils,
  Grouping like fays in swooning trances.

Nature a levee holds for me,
  For I am sorrowful and weary;
Bright birds, pour forth your songs of glee,
  Chirp not one note that soundeth dreary.

In cozy languor on the ground,
  "Lets keep no house" cries snail, slow straying;
When like a brazen trumpet's sound,
  A donkey trilled his doleful braying;

The deer sighs from his forest, "Come
  And join with me in ceaseless roving;"
The beetles wand'ring cheerful hum,
  "Don't ape the ants so labor loving."

Let's have a feast of thought and rhyme,
  Pansy platters, purple and golden;
In cedar bower, 'mid scent of thyme,
  Our goblets lily bells unfolden.

What shall our dishes be for sweets?
  The flow'r with nectar running over,
What if our feasting the queen bee cheats!
  We'll gaily sip the honey'd clover.

Gladiolus seem like blossomed swords,
  While rosebuds peep through veil of mosses,
The sailor frog the streamlet fords
  And corn hangs out her pale green flosses;

Verbenas white and red arrayed,
  Seem fairy knights, a tournament holding,
Or elfin army in grand parade,
  With fluttering banners, and flags unfolding.

The doves are gathering on the roof,
  As if in congress great convening;
The silkworm spins her shining woof,
  The crows the ripened fields are gleaning.

As neighbors met for social talk,
  The grouping quails so noisy clatter,
With chignon'd heads and primping walk,
  They ape our belles, e'en in their chatter.

Her silver lace the spider weaves,
  The linnet in the tall pine singeth,
And high 'mid old oaks shining leaves
  The oriole her cradle swingeth.

While Boss pours forth her milk so white,
  As molten pearls so richly shining;
Pomona, like some wizard sprite,
  The full bunched grapes is deftly twining.

Gooseberries hang like scaly gems,
  Currents as strings of rubies shimmer;
Raspberries grow from emerald stems,
  While from the earth strawberries glimmer;

Passion-vine leaves as fingers spread,
   Like Turkish mosques each flower standeth ;
The roses shake 'neath humming-birds tread,
   As wing'd elves at their portals landeth.

Yon chrysalis, like sculptured tomb,
   With sudden pulse it heaves and shaketh,
And bursting forth as from death's gloom,
   A butterfly to life awaketh,

With velvet wings of dusky brown,
   Spotted with blue and golden rimming,
No empress boasts a fairer gown,
   Or decks her with more gorgeous trimming.

In dreams we'll haste o'er woodland trail,
   Or danger's cliffs with rapture hieing;
Yosemite, to thy weird vale,
   'Tween mammoth mounts so grandly lying.

Thou loved retreat, thy matchless charms,
   Kindled my soul with inspiration
When first you oped your stony arms
   To me an atom of creation.

Thy falls like melted diamond seas,
   As gods were thunders' anvils ringing;
And spreading white tress's to the breeze,
   As naiads from the high cliffs springing.

Thy pond'rous walls and parapets,
  Where tower on tower is lapped or folden,
Thy reaching spires and minarets
  Seem like the works of giants olden.

By Mirror lake we build our camp,
  Where like phantom bark weird firefly saileth,
Where glow-worm trims her mystic lamp,
  As day's amethyst in splendor paleth.

How shall our sylvan board be decked?
  With richest fruits and dainty flowers;
Bring ferns, and pinks, with purple flecked,
  Such as would suit the dryads' bowers.

Where daisies gleam like fallen stars,
  Shall be our carpet's grassy nettings;
And we'll have for branch candelabras,
  Tiger lilies with jetty settings;

Wide-mouthed trumpet beaker shall be
  To quaff the stream where frost-king lingers,
We sip the flood with ecstacy,
  Fresh from touch of his icy fingers.

Back to the actual, the real,
  From Fancy's bright, enraptured roving;
I wake to know and thankful feel,
  I dwell amid the true, the loving,

And listening to the wild bees hum,
  I busy unto his lay respond—
'Mid trials of an earthly home,
  Dream of that glorious world beyond.

* * *

OUR ANGEL BOY.*

One Christmas morn there nestled near my heart,
  A fair-browed babe, just blossomed unto earth;
While voice of praise, and anthem song proclaimed
  The blessed tidings of our Saviour's birth.
My soul was filled with joy unspeakable
  That holy sabbath morn, for gift so sweet;
The day our Lord was born, my babe was given to me—
  This Christmas sits he at the Saviour's feet.

With streaming eyes and whit'ning lips I kneel,
  And humbly cry: "My God, thy will be done!"
Yet 'twas the bitterest sorrow of my life,
  To see death smite our babe, our gentlest one;
And my strong mother-love goes reaching out
  In the far depths of vast eternity,
In search of him, my boy, my precious one,
  Who seems by loss made doubly dear to me.

*Charles Francis Cook—Born Christmas Day, 1870; died October 24th, 1877.

My Savior, take our lamb, our lovely one,
　And fold him safely to thy pitying breast;
After the weary, suffering pangs of death,
　In thy blest home, sweet Jesus, give him rest.
Shall he not 'mong the ransomed dwell with thee?
　To trust thy promise, Oh, give me grace!
To know that, nestling near the great white throne,
　He now beholds our holy Father's face!

But as we count our household daily o'er,
　Still our 'reft hearts will murmur: "We are seven;"
Though at our board there stands a vacant chair,
　One feasts, we know, with angels up in heaven.
Of such thou saidst thy sinless kingdom were,
　And that thy flock should know their Shepherd's voice.
Didst thou not call our loved one to thy fold,
　And bid him in thy Paradise rejoice?

Thou spirit blest!　Thy dying eyes met mine
　In sad farewell.　The ransomed soul revealed,
'T was glorified, in that resplendent gaze,
　Ere life's eclipse thy lids forever sealed.
Oh, gates of pearl! were ye not left ajar,
　That our dear angel might go softly in?
Seraphic hosts! did not your songs of joy
　Welcome our boy, that bore no taint of sin?

A crown of jewels God gave unto me—
　The worthy crown of tender motherhood;

But one was taken back by him who gave,
  Who made all things, and said his work was good.
Was I not worthy of so rare a charge
  As this my gem, that's taken from my crown?
While I in sorrow's sackcloth wrap my heart,
  And in grief's ashes humbly bow me down.

And say: "Almighty God, thy will be done!"
  Trusting the hand that smites will heal and bless.
'Mid clouds of anguish, bow of promise gleams,
  That tells: "I will not leave ye comfortless."
Not comfortless, good Lord, not comfortless;
  Though hearts may ache, and heads in weeping bow,
We know our dear one walks thy shining courts,
  And glory's halo crowns his cherub brow.

MEMORIAL—MY BROTHER.

Upon life's troubled river, a wrecked and shattered vessel,
  Lay tossing so wearily upon the waters wide;
The angry waves around it like battl'ing furies wrestle;
  Who will cut the moorings loose, and guide it o'er the tide?
Ah! who but He, the Lord, Christ, can hush the tempest's
      pinings—
  Can loose the wrecked craft's mooring, and guide it to
      that shore?

We look across the waters, and think we see the shinings
  Of the glory that enwraps thy soul, now and evermore;
And we know our sainted dear ones among that spirit band,
Will welcome thee with gladness unto their beaming strand.

And I'm thinking, I'm thinking, and haplessly I'm weeping,
  While twilight's gloomy shadows across the garden fall—
Of our dear one, who meekly, so placidly lay sleeping,
  Hid 'neath the foldings of the solemn funeral pall,
Of the kindly face there lying—the waxen hands they folded,
  That can ne'er clasp my own in true tenderness again.
The brow so white, and chiseled—the features death had
      moulded,
  To such look of holy calmness, they bear no trace of pain—
Of the cruel pain that slew him, that cut life's cords apart,
And hushed for aye the beating of my gentle brother's heart.

Such mournful days we watched him, weary nights we
      waited,
  In such hopelessness and anguish—agonizing fear,
While every morn seemed gloomy and every hour seemed
      freighted
  With fell-destroyer's message we shudd'ring felt was near;
Oh! wretched time of mourning, of such boding, such dread-
      ing,
  As we saw the whit'ning temples, mark'd the fainting
      breath—
Saw the pale shades waving, and like ghostly moonlight
      spreading,
  O'er lovely brow and features, ghastliness of death;

And we tried with humble faith to think that it was best,
That Christ —pitying Saviour—should call thee home to rest.

We pray to Him, the Holy One; prayed Him as a blessing,
    To take thee from thy suffering, and gather to his fold,
One whose works shone out before him, then, with sad
        distressing,
    We fain had held thee here, when the dews so chill and cold
Came stealing o'er thy forehead, in our anguished sorrow,
    In all thy pain and suff'ring, we fain had held thee here—
From the golden land of promise—the glorious to-morrow—
    While the pearly gates stood open, to that happier sphere;
And thy feet were on the threshold—our frail human love,
Held thee on life's thorny path, from God and Heaven above.

Sweetest anthem-singing linnets, chant from woodland
        bowers,
    While gorgeous flow'rs emblazon hillside and the plain,
And the drowsy owlets' nodding, where twilight's hazing
        lower;
    While wild bees' hum and crickets' chirp mingle choral
        strain,
These blithe voices of glad nature's glorious melody,
    Thou ever seemest to love, oh, brother mine, so, dear;
And as I think, and dream, in memory's imagery,
    Comest thou, with kindly glance, and words of hope
        and cheer;
Thou heaven-inspired soul, who with ever patient care,
My many sorrows soothed, and taught me how to bear.

THE CARNIVAL OF SUMMER.

The Hollyhock her glowing flagon rears,
Pearl blazoned with Night's translucent tears,
    Gleaming with myriad gems;
While mimicing Sol in his noon-day blaze,
The Sunflowers their brazen helmets raise
    High on their stalwart stems.

The Morning Glory holds her beaker up,
And the Pink opens wide her rosy cup,
    A shimmer of glist ning dew;
The Verbenas gather in fay-like band;
The Larkspurs in soldierly rankings stand
    In their coats of army blue.

Like a blushing maid, sudden waked from sleep,
Lo ! the morn looks over yon mountain steep
    And a rosy net work will spin;
At flask of Blue Bell the saucy Wren sipt,
And the Woodpecker chiseled his tiny cript
    And buried the acorn within.

The Marigold flutters her yellow locks,
And the Zephyr's rude caressing mocks,
    With deftest coquetry;
Kissing the lips of the Daisy he'll pass,
As she coyful hides 'mid the tangled grass,
    For a truant lover is he.

Then he danced 'mong the Hawthorn's shim'ring leaves
Where a Spider a shining net work weaves,
     Tangling her silken threads;
And flinging it out in the glittering air,
Oh ! he rent it here, and he rent it there,
     In a thousand gleamy shreds.

He dallied awhile with the Lily white,
As she stood in her bridal robes bedight,
     With their cream-hued satin gloss;
While the Passion Flower reared her chapel shrine,
The Apostles twelve, and the holy sign
     Of the cross, the blessed cross;

And the Tulip tossing her haughty head,
Her purple skirts in the sunshine spread,
     As wooing the Honey Bee;
But the Rose 'neath folds of her pink hued vest
Clasped the traitor knight to her pulsing breast,
     In a dream of ecstasy.

The Humming Bird richest nectar drank
From the Honey-Suckles wine hued tank,
     Flitting from flower, to flower;
And the Rosignol trilled his sweetest plaint,
As hymning to heaven his morning chant,
     From the Elm tree's leafy bower.

Blazoned with jasper, garnet, and gold,
The Butterfly's crimpl'd flounces unfold
    With nonchalant dainty grace;
And with 'broider'd bodice, and royal trail,
A beauteous queen is our stately Quail,
    As she steps with haughty pace.

The Oleander her perfumed censer swings,
And her incense sweet in fragrance flings,
    Scenting the morning air;
While the Violet's fair like saintly eyes
Gaze sweetly up to the eternal skies,
    In seeming faith, and prayer.

See the Lilac raises her plumed head,
And like beaded coral the Sumac red
    Waves in the light of day;
And the Corn shaketh out her amber skeins,
And the Squirrels sport 'mid the rip'ning grains
    In speckled suits of grey.

Lo ! the Cherry blossoms and Apples blow,
Have sheeted the earth like a shroud of snow,
    And Peach's delicate bloom;
O'er the whitened mass so richly spread,
Seem like roses strewn o'er the blessed dead,
    Robed for the solemn tomb.

The Meadow Lark wrapped in her striped coat,
With spotted tippet, and necklaced throat,
          Carrols melifluous songs,
While the Robin in slate-hued Talma drest,
With bright-red apron athwart her breast,
          The choral hymn prolongs.

The sluggish waters all solemnly reach
Like mammoth tongues, up the pebbly beach,
          Shivering their frosty tips;
Where, with endless echoes, the bright shells sound,
And the Sea Gull wheeleth giddily round,
          And into the water dips.

The Buttercups bright in their yellow frocks,
And the dreaming chalice of Four-o'clocks,
          Manzanita's waxen urns,
And the Daffodils, and the Mignonette,
And the flamed-dyed Lily all flecked with jet,
          Carnation that glows, and burns;

The Jasmine, and Myrtle, with odor sweet,
And Orange blossoms so chastely neat,
          The Trumpet so widely blown;
The gorgeons Cactus with stately air,
That as proudly sits in his thorny chair
          As emperor on his throne,

And the nun-like mole in her rayless cell,
That lost to earth's pleasures must drearily dwell,
      In a life of mystery.
The priestly Raven in cassock, and cowl,
The widow'd dove, and monk-like Owl,
      All join in the festive glee.

With carol, and laugh, the glittering rills
Like silver ribbons are belting the hills,
      With glistening silver bands,
While carpeting mountain, valley and plain,
See the glorious Wild flowers choicely lain,
      As painted by angel hands,

The tall Grass waves like billowy seas,
And the Buckeyes, like banners in the breeze,
      Flutter in marshall pride;
Soon the Grapes shall gleam like emerald gems,
And the Currants cluster on their stems,
      Peach don its buckskin hide.

Like lovely mosaic of varied dye,
Yon Dahlia stands, as on minaret high,
      Some gorgeous Moslem tower.
The Peonies in crimson vestments decked,
Geranium by amethyst tinges flecked,
      O'er lowly blossoms tower.

Like a ghostly bark, from the spirit land,
With gossamer sails, and by specters manned,
          A cloud o'er heaven is blown;
While the Linnet her mate to the banquet calls,
Where the Cherries swing their polished balls,
          And the Nectarine rounds its zone,

The spotted Trout slides 'long the streamlet's bank,
Fluttering in many an antic prank,
          As mocking the mermaid's dance,
And feasting upon the tissue-like fly,
That like Goblin Elves on the waters lie.
          Where the brightest sunbeams lance.

See the Ants by base of the forest trees,
All gathered in thriving colonies,
          Their cone-like mansions raise;
That high o'er the puny builder lowers,
Even like Egypt's wonderous towers,
          O'er hosts of ancient days.

Quaint architects too, are the Swallows brown,
As they hastily rear their homely town
          Of wigwams the eaves below;
While the Whip'o-will her plaintive octave sings,
And the Oriole her tiny hammock swings,
          High on the locust bough.

Lo! the wily Hawk, that like dastard foe,
So unerring strikes his treacherous blow,
    And the wasp with stinted waist;
And the deer in his cozy, Lapland wrap,
The Bat in his leather jacket and cap,
    The Rabbit so kindly faced.

And the Cow with wondering, thoughtful mien,
And the young Lambs gamboling on the green,
    The Goats in wandering ranks,
The Gold Finch in his blouse of orange hue,
And the Jays in kilts of bonniest blue,
    Sporting in airy pranks.

In stalactial chambers of the deep
The finny tribes too, this festival keep,
    'Mid grottoes and glistening caves,
Where perchance the Naiads in mystical homes,
Crowned with minaret towers, and coral domes,
    Dwell 'neath the glitt'ring waves,

In a colorless sack, or purple suit,
On the Fig trees nestle the infant fruit,
    Close to the branches prest;
While Strawberries like clustering jewels seem,
And Blackberries in ebon jet-drops gleam.
    On fair earth's verdant breast.

The Gooseberry as globe of amber swings,
The Elder her pebbly fruitage brings,
        The Ivy spreadeth her leaves;
The Canary sporteth in lemon surtout,
The Mocking Bird whistles his liquid flute,
        Her basque the Silk-Worm weaves.

The Gage and Apricot soon shall come,
With the Nectarine and delicious Plum,
        And bedeck the orchard trees;
The Apple shall ripen, as by magic spells,
And the Pears shall dangle like golden bells,
        Swung by the wandering breeze.

The bright fields glow with wakening charms,
And the spinach spreads her brawny palms—
        Celery like tapers stands;
The Peas open wide their ripening pods,
And the Beans hang out their dangling rods,
        Like mystic finger wands.

The stilted Grasshopper goes hurrying by,
While like rubies spilt the Lady Bugs lie
        'Mong leaves in the sunny light;
The Beetles in armor of golden mail,
And the downy Miller so fair and frail,
        Is cloaked in dimity white.

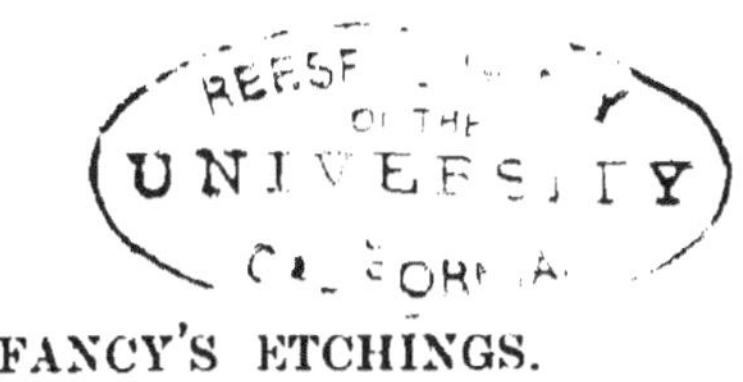

See the Kildee bird that with gestures light,
Like a Peri Nymph, or a fairy sprite,
          Skips where the brooklets gleam;
And with airy motions, quivers and flirts,
And giddily dippeth her trailing skirts,
          Into the shining stream.

As the crimson splendors of sunset pale,
The laced wing'd Moths in the twilight sail,
          'Mong hazy beams of the west;
And look like distant ships far out at sea,
That the tiniest Moats seem but to be,
          On ocean's heaving breast.

The Cricket in habit of dusty brown,
And the Katy-did robed in her silken gown,
          Her tunic of daintiest green;
All plaintively join in the choral hymn,
While the stars their vestal tapers trim,
          'Round Night the Ethiope Queen.

The Labelula wooed to the Poppies nest,
All lazily swaying, swooned to rest,
          Lulled by her breath to sleep;
And never awoke as he dreamily heard
The psalm of the Vesper's twilight bird
          Ring through the forest deep.

The full-eyed Frog, in his mottled sack,
With silver facings and streaked back,
    As an Evil Geni seems;
While in Elfin watch-fires through the night
The Glow Worm kindles her beacon light
    In vivid, flashing beams.

The milky-way spreadeth o'er heaven's floor,
As with diamond sands it were dusted o'er,
    Or jewel pennant unfurled;
Lo! like fiery snake yon meteor ran,
And constellations fill His wond'rous plan
    Who formed each rolling world.

When the flowers, and herd, and kine rejoice,
Oh! shall we not join with jubilant voice
    To greet this lovely time;
Thy carnival, sweet Summer, season fair,
Sure the Seraphs are singing in the air,
    To hail thy golden prime.

LAUGH AND BE GAY.

Laugh, laugh and be gay,
Yes, laugh while ye may,
  And ne'er nurse the demon of sorrow.
Though clouds of to-day
May dim the sun's ray
  'Twill as brightly shine on the morrow.

Let no thought of ill,
Mirth's carolling still;
  Ne'er harbor the spectre of sadness,
List, the joy-shouting trill
Of the twittering rill,
  Is mur'ring forever of gladness.

Aye morns rosy light
Is followed by night,
  In nature's mysterious changing.
So some evil sprite,
Earth's friendship may blight,
  For some hearts are given to ranging.

With sorrow's alloy
Ne'er pleasures destroy,
  Nor o'ershadow the beauty of earth;
Though vexations annoy,
Aye revel in joy,
  And still cherish the spirit of mirth.

The present ne'er doom.
To visions of gloom;
  All forebodings of misery spurn;
Ne'er dream of the tomb,
In the heart's freshen'd bloom,
  But with joy to futurity turn.

Ah! ne'er have fear,
But be of good cheer,
  And the cup of contentment still quaff;
While those that are dear
Are hovering near,
  To join in the innocent laugh!

O'er the sky's stormy plain,
Formed of sunshine and rain,
  The bright bow of promise is given;
So joy and so pain—
Form a glittering chain,
  That anchors our hopes up in heaven.

Not jewels, or gold,
Nor riches untold,
  Can e'er purchase that Kingdom above;
In hunger and cold,
'Mong poverty's fold,
  Jesus seeketh the Lambs of his love.

Sad mortal, ne'er spurn
The beings that' yearn
  To brush from thy pathway the clouds.
But gratefully turn
To the bosoms that yearn
  To soothe when the spirit is bowed.

The best friends are those
Who comfort our woes,
  And not they who but share in our cheer.
Where the brightest light shows,
Moths bask in its glows,
  But a friend in night's sorrow is near.

'Tis well he who heeds
Faith and good deeds,
  And his mite with the needy aye shares.
Yes, though thy good seeds
Are smothered by weeds,
  Our God knoweth who soweth the tares!

SOMEBODY'S DAUGHTER.

Somebody's daughter, a thing of clay,
On slab at a Morgue helplessly lay,
No one to claim her the live long day.

Somebody's eyes had been wet with tears,
And somebody's heart had ached with fears,
As mother look'd back o'er the hapless years.

When her child went forth a bride forsooth,
With cheeks ablush, with radiant youth,
Plighting her troth with the vow of truth.

But time sped on, and as swift years ran,
The bridegroom forgot the marriage ban,
The youth had become a harden'd man.

The heartless dastard, heedlessly hurl'd,
A helpless wife, alone on the world
Where river of life giddily swirl'd.

And her nut brown hair, and eyes of blue,
Were sold for bread, but nobody knew,
But one who lured her from virtue true.

With blandishing word of pay for toil,
A simple copyist, naught to soil
Her lovely hands—but the serpents' coil.

Branded his victim day after day,
'Till woke to fear as tigress at bay,
To find she'd stray'd from the beaten way.

With none to help her, no one to care,
She woke in a crazy, mad despair,
To feel she was trapped in a demon's lair.

And she took the life, a good God gave,
With none to tell of Him that could save,
'Ere she lay at Morgue for pauper's grave.

No christian sister to pour in light,
Of the home, where souls are washed so white,
By a Saviour's blood from sin's dark blight.

Though steeped so deep in its black decay,
Dear Jesus, forgive such souls—astray,
While at the Morgue they friendlessly lay.

THE PICTURE.

Come Artist, now paint me a picture
  Of my lady, dainty and fair,
Just catch me her loveliest dimples,
  The light on her soft golden hair;
The rose on her cheek but the faintest,
  That line for the exquisite nose,
And the lips delicious twin berries,
  As they meet in such placid repose.

Mark that throat like statue of marble,
    And those eyes with heaven's own tinge,
See those lids, the whitest of snowflakes,
    With lashes of long, silken fringe;
And those hands, ah! can you e'er paint them?
    So matchless are they in their form;
The mould of the beautiful figure,
    Oh! would that to life it could warm.

Now catch you the gleam of the sunset,
    That lies 'cross the finely turned wrist,
Then brows so bewitchingly arching,
    And the ears like shells, do you list?
Like Nectar, just pour o'er the canvas
    The ring of her magical laugh!
Now Artist, of charms so enchanting,
    I find you can paint me but half.

But her song like lark at the morning,
    In quaver, and extatic trill;
Could you paint me? but oh! I am dreaming,
    My fancy her beauties so fill.
That head's symmetrical posing;
    That look of Madona, or saint.
But the beautiful soul of my lady,
    Only angels in heav'n can paint,

NEVER A BRIDE.

'Twas not one hundred year's ago,
There came at twilight's ruddy glow,
Pure as a tiny flake of snow,
   A baby fair,
   With golden hair,
A gift from heav'n to earth below.

Deep in cushions of snowy white,
Swath'd as in robes of pearly light,
This lovely, fairy, dimpled sprite,
   Thus lay in state,
   At door of fate,
As evening sank in arms of night.

She, the mother, a very child,
Through raining tears tenderly smil'd
O'er type of him who so beguiled
   And led astray
   From virtue's way
Her blameless life he'd so defiled.

Hers the bitter lot that comes to some,
With promise fair that he would come,
When foreign lands he'd cease to roam,
   What e'er betide,
   She'd be his bride;
Very queen of his princely home.

But alas ! when twilight's deep'ning gray
Was holding sunset's glare at bay,
She in narcotic stupor lay,
                    With face of shame
                    He stealthy came,
And stole the babe from her arms away.

Yes, came with tiger's stealthy tread,
And stole his child from its snowy bed,
While mother lay as one that's dead.
                    Out in the night
                    He took his flight,
As pale moon ghostly shadows spread.

Away in its robes of splendid state,
There in basket at foundling's gate
He left it there to an unknown fate,
                    His baby fair
                    With golden hair;
So his soul may plead at heaven too late.

Then away o'er mighty deep he sped,
With stony heart and panther tread,
While the mother lay cold and dead.
                    With face so white,
                    That awful night,
While angels were watching over head.

She who nursed her so sadly sigh'd
As the waxen hands together she tied,
And said, "yes 'twere better she died,
      Than in disgrace
      The world to face;
A mother, yet never a bride.

Women with tender hands outreach,
With woman's tongue in tender speech
Tell such, God's saving love can reach
      The saddest heart
      That bears sin's smart;
That he the blackest soul can bleach.

TO J. J. B., MY BROTHER.

Do not forget me if grief's storms of anguish
  Come sweeping o'er my path like wintry blast,
Ah! no, thy true affection cannot languish,
  But like the sunlight, let it ever cast
Its glory on my way—a heav'nly blessing
  To gild the present—and the future light
Amid life's ills, no matter how distressing,
  Still let it live, like one lone star at night.
When black'ned clouds, the skies in gloom are veiling,
  So, so, to me amid the pangs of woe,

Let thy love beam, oh! never, never failing
  In its deep tenderness— shall it not be so
May I not from the past, thy future kindness
  Still fearless trust—nor ought my fond faith break,
Not with that wild hope, with its weird-like blindness,
  That trusting the untried, at last will wake
To falsehood--as thou'st proved, so be forever,
  Nor cast my love away as worthless, weak.
'Mid all life's ills, let nought our fondness sever,
  But heart to heart, for aye in kindness speak.

SUSPENSE.

I sit at my wheel and try to spin,
As the tides go out, and tides come in,
    Ah! sorrow, ah! woe is me.
I list in vain and my cheeks grow pale,
While watching to see the snow white sail,
    That wafts my lover from sea.

I sigh as I walk on pebbly beach,
Where the mighty breakers seem to reach,
    As great monsters after me,
And with eager haste, and trembling hand,
I hurriedly trace on shining sand,
    The name that was mine to be.

And I sadly shade my yearning sight,
From dazzling glare of the sunny light,
				As I look far out to sea.
Each rising swell of the bounding wave,
Seemeth to me but a mounded grave,
				Between my lover and me.

There's a mast, and keel, and splintered deck,
And broken spars of a shattered wreck,
				Afar up the pebbly shore.
And giddily whirls my crazy brain,
As I weep for fear that never again,
				Will he come as once of yore,

Yet better—better that he were lost,
And his bark by mighty tempests tost,
				And sunk in a stormy sea.
Than ever to me he recreant prove,
And break his vows of eternal love,
				A traitor to me—Ah! me.

He said e'er the pearl white moon should ride,
Like a silver boat on the placid tide,
				In a twelve months time that he,
With gifts from many a foreign land,
Would come and claim my bonny hand,
				As his wife for aye to be.

But he haunteth me in dreams at night,
With a ghastly face, in ghostly light,
          He comes and looketh at me.
And his white lips ever seem to knell,
A sad, oh! a solemn, sad farewell,
          Mid roar of a stormy sea;

THE MAGIC GLASS.

'Mong legends old and weird romances,
That so the dreary mind entrances,
                    My lay hath part;
A strange, wild tale of wizard power,
Of Ghostly Elves, and midnight hour,
                    And magic art.

Of an old Castle quaint and hoary,
Of Goblin spell, a mystic story,
                    It doth betray.
'Twas Hallow-e'en when sprite, and fairy,
And haunting ghouls so wierd, and airy,
                    Come forth they say.

A bright-eyed maid had vowed to clamber,
Up to the turrets highest chamber,
       Alone perchance,
And there her own sweet face but viewing,
In an old glass—the wizard suing,
       For one quick glance,

Of him who here her future sharing,
Would win her heart—with reckless daring,
       The glass was sought.
The battling storm with fearful shouting,
Raged wild and fierce, and seemed as scouting
       Her frenzied thought.

The grim owl through the woodland skimming,
Shrieked in the midnight's dusky grimming,
       Like Banshee's cry.
The ship-like moon, tost worriedly
Through seas of clouds, that hurriedly
       Dashed through the sky.

Like twisting tongues in fiery gleamings,
Forked light'nings shed their lurid beamings.
       In serpent trails.
In gaudy flame of brazen sheeting,
The glowing columns fast and fleeting,
       Now shines, now pales.

By cannon thunders earth seem'd riven,
As if the battlements of heaven,
     Stay legion storms,
While foaming waves were swiftly driven,
The groaning trees held up to heaven
     Their shattered forms.

And there within that chamber lonely,
Like rigid statue seemed she only,
     So moveless stands.
Her bright eyes in the mirror gazing,
While round her form a misty hazing,
     Now wreathes and bands,

Her slender figure quaint entombing,
While a faint sense of ghostly glooming,
     About her seems.
One look—one look of him the chosen,
To bless her lot so fixed, and frozen,
     Her white face gleams;

As far and near with boistrous swelling,
The shouting winds swept round that dwelling,
     Like wail of care,
Like stars, and sunshine wove together,
Or shining web of netted ether,
     Gleam'd all the air.

While near her frantic laughs were ringing.
And sounds of strange sepulchral singing,
     And sigh and moan
And low within the mirror gleaming,
A ghastly face reflects in seeming,
     Besides her own,

And be it goblin', sprite, or devil,
Oh! terror, sure some deed of evil,
     The place has curs't
Some demon here, or ghostly brightness
Hath power a mid this gloomy nightness,
     The tomb to burst.

Such fearful sounds like human wailing,
Rang through those halls, Yet still unfailing,
     She listless clings,
Intently in the mirror gazing,
While tones sweep by her sense amazing,
     Of countless wings.

Her heart its wonted throbbing ceasing,
Seemed as it were her soul releasing,
     In terror's might,
While aye upon her anxious hearing,
Low voices whispered ever nearing,
     In tones so light.

Lorene! Lorene! all softly naming,
While sneering faces mocking, shaming,
    In phantom throngs,
While bursts of music near her ringing,
Seemed fiends in bachanalian singing,
    Of demon songs.

Past twelve o'clock the church chimes tell,
And waking as from some mad spell,
    She lists in fear.
Yet naught save the wild owlets notes,
Upon the dim night ether floats,
    To greet her ear.

The spell dissolved—the frighted maid,
With heaving chest, and sore dismayed,
    The chamber left.
While at her side a figure tall,
Goes on through each high winding hall,
    'Till nigh bereft,

She gains the throng, each gay one chiding
Her thoughtful mood, yet she still hiding
    Her secret's might.
No word of what she saw in seeming,
Escaped those lips the sounds, the gleaming,
    That met her sight.

Her sister's prayer she listless heedeth,
Though Bella the cause of mystery pleadeth,
                    Her secret slept.
In her poor heart so darkly wrestling,
Like viper near a linnet nestling,
                    The knowledge slept.

Months past, yet a strange presence bound her,
A phantom being linger'd round her,
                    From hour, to hour.
T'was with her in the sunny light,
T'was with her in her dreams at night,
                    The blasting power.

One day into the village came
A stranger, none might tell his name,
                    But tales there were.
Of heaping wealth, of countless gold,
Report the tale hath eager told,
                    From ear to ear.

There came a night when earth seem'd laden
With the transfigured light of Aiden,
                    Heav'ns atmosphere,
Earth seemed as swooned in mystic trancing
As on the green for country dancing,
                    The throngs draw near,

And swirl as in a world of dreaming,
While moonlight so delusive seeming,
                    Rained hallowed light.
As nectar we had sipped and draining,
And drank as some delicious raining,
                    Of jewels bright.

And there the maid and stranger met,
Her gaze scarce on his features set,
                    Ere that wierd sight,
Came swiftly on her startled mind,
And seem'd with the same pow'r to bind,
                    Of that wild night.

Strange beauty had he, and a pow'r
Was round her cast from hour to hour,
                    Linking her soul.
All, all would shun him save the maid,
On her some fearful spell was laid,
                    Naught could control.

Strange meetings had they too, I ween,
Where never human form was seen,
                    In times gone by.
In a wild dell as legends say,
The haunt of goblin, sprite and fay
                    As eve drew nigh.

Oh ! were he fiend, or were he mortal ?
Or spirit, that had burst Death's portal ?
      To wander here,
While at his side a silent rapture,
Would hold her ev'ry sense in capture,
      A speechless fear.

All loves were lost in this mad one,
Ah! could she know a demon spun
      This Hade's spell.
This mystic charm around her heart,
How she would snap the cords apart,
      And rend the spell,

But she could list poor Bella's pleading,
And all so helpless never heeding
      Her wailing cry.
Sickened that sister from the woe,
That seem'd o'er her this spell to throw,
      Of mystery.

And on her brow the damps of death,
Lay chill, and cold, the hurried breath.
      Spoke sudden doom.
Told the chill presence near her now,
Yet Lorene kept her plighted vow,
      At midnight gloom.

For she had promised, ere dawned the light,
To meet, and wed, the mystic knight,
                    In that wierd tower.
At midnight hour what e'er betide,
She'd vowed, she'd sworn to be his bride,
                    At ghostly hour.

Yes, she must fly, some numbing trance,
Lulls every sense—e'en though perchance,
                    Ne'er to return.
And that sister's face never to view,
Yet must she fly for true, true, true,
                    Her heart throbs yearn,

To him, though blindly false to all,
That else were dear—All loves must fall,
                    And fade away.
Before this wild, distracting dream,
This will-o' wisp's delusive gleam,
                    That o'er her lay.

With wild enchantment so intense,
A charm was binding every sense,
                    With fetters grim.
And she has sought the castle tower,
To meet her love at midnight hour,
                    And wed with him.

The phantom power that bound her life,
To conscience dumb, was there no strife,
                        No pang of woe?
With duty, and with passion's test,
Within that once so sinless breast,
                        Ah! no, Ah! no.

Lo! to the mirror her glances raising,
The same dark eyes in hers are gazing,
                        In soft reply.
'Mid sounds of strife and cries of pain,
The same wild faces gleam again,
                        As eye, met eye.

But Bella's soul from its temple leaping,
Beside her form is lightly sweeping;
                        A shadowy mist.
Like filmy clouds of gleamy brightness,
Or seraph robed in spotless whiteness,
                        Her brow it kist.

She lists, and low upon her calling,
'Tis he, her love, her soul appalling,
                        With pallid face.
Again she lists its mystic sounding,
'Tis he! 'tis he! and wildly bounding
                        To his embrace.

She forward springs—between them glooming,
A white and ghastly form is looming,
            With face of woe;
The pale lips speak, ''Oh! sister stay,''
And the phantom fled like mist away,
            Or drift of snow.

The spell was broken, that angel soul,
Had rent the demon power's control,
            For aye and aye.
With throbbing pulse and heaving chest,
And heart and mind so sad distressed,
            In wild dismay,

She sought fond Bella's bower now,
Hapless at last to tell her woe,
            So sore amazed;
But cold in death lay that gentle form,
Which vainly to life she strove to warm,
            Till almost craz'd.

That soul hath passed from earth forever,
Ne'er to return, Oh! never, never,
            To all its pain.
Could they e'er meet, would she e'er win
A place in heaven? For this foul sin
            Plead she in vain?

To be forgiven—yes, God aye hears
The sinner's cry—repentant tears
        Can wash out sin,
Are far more precious than the gems
That deck the Seraph's diadems,
        And heaven will win.

THE AUTUMN RAIN.

In glad refrain,
'Gainst window pane,
     Comes tripping,
The dashing rain,
In sparkles bright,
Of chrystal light.
     There dripping,
All through the night.

So gailey tost,
Like Fairy host,
     There rapping,
In darkness lost.
With merry din,
For entrance in.
     Aye tapping,
They whirl and spin.

Each slides and slips,
Like finger tips,
    There drumming.
Or sparkling drips,
They bound and leap,
Or glide and creep,
    Aye humming.
In chorus deep.

Like cheery throng,
The whole night long,
    They clatter,
A merry song
Like ghostly eyes,
In sad surprise,
    They spatter,
Each glistening pane.

Against the glass,
A glittering mass,
    They shimmer,
Or fade and pass,
Or shine and cling;
As living thing.
    And glimmer,
Like pearls astring.

All through the night,
In starry light,
　　　There gleaming,
As diamonds bright,
Oh ! welcome rain,
Against the pane,
　　　Come streaming,
With glad refrain.

A PHILANTHROPIST'S DREAM,

But yester e'en I dreamt a vision quaintly strange,
　Beside a water's edge there stood a woman fair,
In pearl white robes—so chastely beautiful was she,
　As round her like a mantle, coiled her lovely hair,
Like web of sunshine; while noiseless upon the tide
　A brazen trumpet fell and floated to her feet,
Which, stooping, she grasped up, and pressing to her lips,
　Sent forth a blast that rang in cadence sweet;
When on the shining flood there suddenly appeared
　Innumerable tiny fish, like flakes of snow,
And each was spouting forth myriads of precious gems,
　That in translucent gleams of splendor glow,
And in their midst fair flowery wreaths dropt down,
　And shining golden crowns came floating on the wave,

While I, amazed, did anxious ask this being fair,
  What meaneth this? and she in accents soft and grave,
Replied, the snow white fish bespeak the conscience clear;
  The gems, they shimmer forth with deeds of kindness rife,
Are typical; the crowns and wreaths image to thee,
  The just rewards that wait thee in the spirit life;
Then falteringly I said, what emblemist thou
  So beautiful of mien, so holy and so pure?
In soft response she spake, I symbol heavenly love
  To all the just of heart, who patiently endure.
Then rouse bowed hearts for glory crowns are waiting ye.
  Work on, work on, and bear in sorrow and in pain;
For the bright heaven that surely beckoneth thee,
  Where misery and wrong can blight no lives again.

VARIED FATES.

How long, oh Lord, must I a pilgrim go?
  O'er mountain crags that pierce my bleeding feet
O'er cliffs that bend, O'er fearful chasms below,
  Through fetid marsh, and city's busy street;
Wearied and tired, in sorrow and in pain,
  Like Israel's Pilot, rest not night or day,
Fleeing from justice, while lifes an endless lane,
  Of haunting ghosts, a cheerless sunless way,
But looking up, I hear thee, murmur go!

'Till faith lights up for thee Earth's wilderness
With my forgiveness sweet amid thy woe,
  Rest is with me, and I cán heal and bless.

How long, Oh Lord, must I with tired hands
  Plow endless fields that others harvest reap ?
While I on chaff can feed, view endless bands
  Heaping with food for others, while I weep
For hunger—see fruitage of my toil
  That but enriches those that sit at ease.
While I must plow and plant for them the soil,
  Nor ever rest me, fanned by cooling breeze;
'Neath arid suns, but heated waters drink,
  For taste of icy founts my master sips,
Nor dare to loiter round its cooling brink
  To press one shining drop to parching lips.

How long, Oh! Lord, shall I with aching sight,
  Guide the swift needle, that my babes may live ?
Is life for me a task, a scene of blight ?
  Hast thou no better fate dear Lord to give,
Or have I sinned ? What is this, my sin ?
  A drunkard's wife—and these his babes uncared;
Is his sin mine ? Can not my prayers yet win
  Forgiveness e'en for him, that he be spared
From wrath to come ? If in true penitence that he
  Kneel, as I kneel, thou canst his soul make white;
With thy dear love, Oh! Christ, all power is given thee
  The blind in sin to give redeeming sight.

How long, Oh! Lord, shall I that her so wronged,
　　Be haunted, reproachful, by her dying face,
My nightly dreams by vengeful demons thronged,
　　Is there for me no secret hiding place?
To flee from conscience scorpions—and from thee—
　　To put myself away—Oh! let the rocks but fall
And crush me—let my soul die out and be
　　As it had never been. Thou who reignest o'er all
Power'd to give, and take of life, blot out this soul of mine.
　　And yet methinks I see her bow at mercy's seat,
And plead for me. Vengeance, my God, is thine;
　　Thou to repentance givest forgiveness sweet.

How long, Oh! Lord, must I bear stripes and blows,
　　And be the gibe and jeer of men of high estate?
For when their waste I beg, they bid me go
　　Nor dare to rest me at their palace gate;
Hear me, Oh! Lord, and give me unbegged bread,
　　Nor let my children cry with hungry need,
I hear thee say, " They who the wine press tread,
　　Shall be partakers of the wine," that ox be freed
From muzzle when he treads the corn, yet as of old
　　Man's barns are full, his grains like billows roll
Teach him dear Lord, the poor are of thy fold,
　　That thou this night could'st ask of him his soul.

How long, Oh! Lord, within a den of crime,
　　Shall I drag out a life of sin and shame?

Is there for me my God! no end of time,
  No end of Earth, and sneering human blame?
Is there no voice to speak, and bid me rise,
  No one to point for me the better ways?
Must I in shame, aye, hide from womans' eyes
  And still be woman—should she not strive to raise
Her kind, though they be fallen—my God!
  Is it not best o'er social gulf she reach her hand,
To raise and save, nor strike with smiting rod?
  But teach the pathway to the better land.

How long, Oh! Lord, shall they, who thy poor feed,
  Visit thy prisoned sick—afflicted ones?
Scatter abroad thy holy gospel seed;
  Live lives as blameless as the noonday sun,
Yet bear reproach—from scandal's fetid breath
  That like some festering pool pours forth its stench,
Breeding diseases foul and horrid death.
  From trials such as these patient spirits wrench
And show the world that they're by liars scourged,
  Nor let the blackening tongue thy chosen shame,
E're the poluting floods above them surge,
  Reach forth dear Christ, and save a guiltless name.

How long, Oh! Lord, from 'neath thy throne in heaven,
  Shall we cry out the unavenged souls?
Thy Prophets, saints, who forth from Earth were driven
  In martyrs deaths—Thou whose power controls,

Who worlds from nothing built, climes, lands and seas
  And fruitage fair, and herb and blossom sweet;
And gavest to man, the ingrate, blest with these;
  Yet ne'er gave place of rest to Jesus feet,
But him destroyed with cruel, cruel death,
  Who unoffending died on Calvary,
And led the way to heaven, the gospel saith,
  Vengeance is thine, Oh! Lord, so let it be.

TIME AND THE SEASONS.

I.

Like Peris fair, with foreheads serene,
Came skipping along with garlands green,
Two glowing nymphs, in aerial dance.
With laugh and song, at their witching glance,
All earth revives as each gaily show'rs
Around her a fairy gift of flowers
While Flora is scat'ring o'er hill and dell,
On the streamlet's banks, by wood and fell.
The lovely sprites, with wooing smile,
Young Spring doth the rosy gems beguile,
As she warbles to each a song of bliss
Of the balmy dews and zephyr's kiss;

Mailed in his armor of shining gold,
How the lover sun shall their charms enfold,
How he'd paint their breast's with the glowing dyes,
The rainbow banners across the skies;
But the lowly violet should wear the hue,
Pilfered from heaven's resplendent blue.
The ripples chirp forth in cheerful mood,
The rills sing out from the forest wood.
All nature the cup of joy may quaff,
And the earth resounds like a merry laugh;
And 'mid the boughs and leaflets green,
Time's spectral figure was ever seen.

II.

Till with rounded form and rosy lip,
Where god's might ambrosial nectar sip,
Came the Season's Queen and nature smiled
On precious gifts of her favorite child,
As she jewel'd earth with flow'r and leaf,
And the furrowed hills—like brow where grief
Hath left her trace—locked gladly forth,
'Neath emerald crests, from south to north
Her praises rung, their anthems trilling,
The birds the air with joy were filling;
Beauty awakens at her very breathing,
Forest and bower in splendor wreathing;
And, Lo! wherever her footsteps tread,

A spell of glory is sweetly shed;
Insects pipe from their covert of leaves,
The crickets sing from the cottage eaves;
The spiders their lace-like webbings launch,
Netting its maze from branch to branch.
All that is lovely awakes to life,
The earth and air with her gifts are rife.
Gaily she hies o'er the blooming land,
While ever the spectral warning hand
Still pointeth to where the zephyr's sing
The wailing dirge of departed Spring.

III.

But stately Autumn comes marching by,
There's blight in the breath of his chilly sigh,
In his hand a ripened sheaf he bears,
Wreathed on his wither'd brow he wears
A shriveled branch—no flow'rs are springing—
A cluster of luscious fruit is clinging
Round his sturdy form, as merrily
He tears the leaves from the blighted tree.
Vertumnus* is bearing a gleaming store
Of purple grapes, their juices pour
Out on the sombre earth; but no smile ye trace,
No token of joy on her wrinkled face,

---

*Etruscan God—wine and fruits were his peculiar gifts.

No thankful voice from her heart is won
For the precious gifts of her wanton son,
But demons of tempest spring to birth,
The wild winds laugh in bacchanal mirth
Till she quakes in dread. But, like kindly eyes
In seeming pity, the cloudy skies
Weep o'er all nature thus bereft
Of the gems sweet Spring and Summer left;
While marches Autumn with kingly stride,
O'er hill and vale, o'er land and tide;
Yet still, 'mid the haughty monarch's train,
Time's spectral figure was seen again.

IV.

But like warrior vet'ran, Winter appears—
On his ghastly face the frozen tears
Gleam in the light of the noonday beams,
While with icy fetters he chains the streams;
On, onward, tramping o'er land and sea,
While the billows shout in boisterous glee,
Slow moves his blasted figure along
With snowy locks—though firm and strong
Was his giant stride—his glazing breath
Shackled the rills, while blight and death
Were seen wherever his footsteps trod,
From forest oak to the daisied sod.
With frosty fingers he burnish'd the stars

'Till they shim'ring quaked on their flaming cars;
And lo! on the bough where the green leaves hung
His jewels the icy chieftain strung;
While Apollo rained in fiery gleams
His burning glances, yet chill'd the beams
Ere to the earth they had won their flight;
And brightly glowing, the orb of night
Gazed sadly down;—as on went the train
The breeze seemed chanting a funeral strain,
And still Time's spectral figure wends
Yet pointing where earth and season ends.

THE CONVENT.

Vulcan at dawn, from his red furnace in the East,
Rolls out great hoops of light to girdle land and sea,
Still higher and higher rush the glowing flames,
Till, from his blazing forge, he wheels the red hot sun,
Like a live coal seething upon the breast of heaven,
Fanned by the cooling zephyrs of the morn.
Dismal and solemn, in the rich sunlight,
Loom the convent walls—like a dull casket—
As seeming to defy the outward world
With the too precious treasury within.
Couldst look within and mark that queenly form,

Moving in stately majesty 'mid the throng
Of melancholy nuns.   'Tis she, the Abbess
Of that holy sisterhood.

      There are still
Traces of beauty on that time worn face;
But years have passed since first she sought those walls,
And she hath no fellowship with the world.
A being of whom we feel a sacred awe,
Seeming to hold no kindred with the earth,
But, Oh! what various emotions stir
In every bosom there.   While some in quiet,
In holy peace throb but with thoughts of heav'n,
Others there were whose every heart-pulse
Seemed as the dirge-like, funeral knell
Of crushed affections, and of blighted youth.
For there were broken hearts shrouded therein,
Many a prayer breathed before that sacred shrine,
Laden with sighs for peace and hope departed.
Oft bearing a Name that had been prized for years,
Up to the mighty throne of God,

      One came there
Beautiful as Hebe, with cheeks of rose,
With matchless form and brow of lily whiteness,
But sorrow soon stole the rose-hue from her cheek,
And dimmed the brightness of those starry eyes.
Doomed by her sire to Convent's lifeless gloom,
For loving, 'gainst his will, one by him abhor'd.

8

As lightning fells the tree, so swept his rage,
Severing those hearts forever.

                    Lorenzo
The loved, and lost, a maniac became,
While she, in orisons, poured forth her woe,
But one day summon'd to that sire's view,
Nor dreaming why—with throbbing heart she gained
The grate that buried her from the outward world,
Smiling with demon joy in her wan face,
He announced the tidings of Lorenzo's death,
An instant she stood with agony transfixed,
Then from the foldings of her sable habit
A poignard drew and plunged it in her heart.
With eager haste he strove to stay the deed,
But vain, the high grating rose between,
Defying effort.
                    And senseless she fell,
While from her wounded side the life blood-flow'd
A crimson stream upon the snowy pave.
Hapless he gazed and lists return of life,
But soon they came and bore her from his sight.
Never again might he look on that face,
Or clasp unto his heart his murdur'd child;
No, not even in death.

                    Lo! like prison'd dove,
Sighed there still one Nora, also Novice,
Yet in the flush of youth, ere the soul hath felt

The sorrowing the bitterness of earth,
Striving to check the joyous throbbing of her heart.
And bow in penitence before her God,
But seeming 'mid that throng of gloomy nuns
Like to a fleecy cloud 'mid a blacken'd host,
So unfit the glowing beauty of that face,
Not meek with piety, but ever beaming
In artless, childlike innocence and truth.
She was an orphan; had been prisoned there
By a base guardian, who, subtle, scheming,
Grasp'd her inheritance.   Before the world
Mourning her dead, and laid at rest.
And soon she sought companionship with one,
A firm devotee of that holy sisterhood,
One who'd dwelt there from girlhood's early years.
This sister kind held pious converse oft
With a young friar.   He her brother was,
And came to her to hold communion blest,
That he might win his tempted soul from sin.
For he was young, and pleasure ever seem'd
To lure him in her train—his priesthood mock.
And Nora, day by day, look'd on that forehead high,
And listened the music of that tender voice,
Oft meeting his rapid glance.   Till at last
A kindred feeling rose in their young hearts,
And those convent walls became to her
A hated dungeon.

　　　　　　　　　　For he had cast off
All his priestly bonds, nor there might entrance find.
And she had promised she would be his bride
At the appointed time.

　　　　　　　　　　And Nora
Waited at the midnight hour,
Fearful and patient, there upon her knees
In prayer and tears, beseeching heaven's aid,
With flushing cheeks and heart of truest love.

　　　　　　　　　　Rising in sudden haste,
She gained the outer door, drew back the bolts,
And noiseless gliding through the dim, dark path,
The garden wall soon reached, where Juan waited,
An instant paused as if in penitence,
Then grasps the cord he flings and slow ascends,
And sobbing, springs into her lover's arms.
Within a sombre garb he wraps her form,
Hiding in its deep folds her snowy robes;
And soon before the good priest of the town,
They breathed the vows that bound two hearts in one.
Ere yet the moon had sank, morn's sun arose,
Clothed in his golden robes, flinging athwart
The toiling waters a beamy network,
While from the bay sailed out the speeding ship
Which bore away those unit hearts forever.
Within that cloister home at early dawn,
The sacred throng for holy mass assembled;

But the young devotee came not.   In vain
They searched.   Her gloomy cell was tenantless,
And she, the novice fair, was now a bride.
But those high walls still hid a broken heart;
A girl with large dark eyes and pallid brow,
Whose mournful glances ever seemed to beam
Some speechless agony.
                              Often at times,
Her cheek would dye as the quick blush of morn,
And then 'twould fade, as faints the Northern lights,
And her wan features would again assume
The same fixed and marble-like expression.
But the caged bird will droop if nourished long,
Beneath the covering of eternal night;
And so she died, and there were none to mourn;
The past soon shall be forgotten.   None knew
Her tale—for seldom the pale lips parted,
Except in prayer.
                          Now before the altar lies
The frozen wreck of that once lovely being,
Through the dim aisles, dirge-like tones are stealing,
'Tis mass for the departed earth-sick soul.
Peace, let her rest, disturb not by a sound
That calm repose—let not a zephyr's breath
Sweep o'er that quiet face where silence reigns.
Sorrow hath sadden'd that now pulseless heart,
Tears dimmed those eyes—such tears as Angels weep.
Let music's plaint be still—let not a voice
Give forth one thrilling tone.

> Behold! she sleeps.
And lo! the sleep of death.
> Peace! let her rest;
Ye may not bid the wither'd flow'r to bloom,
Ye may not bid the tuneless bird to sing;
Ye may not wake the dead.   No voice hath pow'r,
The loved of Heaven, the blessed, back to win.
Ye may not call the immortal here to dwell,
Let not a sound awake to mar this quiet,
For lo! the dead, the pulseless dead, are here.

A LAY FOR THE SEASON.

Hushed is the rivulet's gleesome song
No longer the streamlet sweeps along
    In summer's golden light ;
The frozen waters lie fixed and deep,*
While Heaven's tireless sentinels keep
    Their watches through the night.

List the voice of Boreas grieving !
And see, the frosty elves are weaving
    Their fret-work for the trees!

---

* I refer to the climate of my late home, New York, where the poor suffer fearfully in winter.

Earth's gorgeous bloom hath faded now,
The leaflet's withered on the bough,
    Kissed by the chilly breeze.

But lo! the storm-winged, ponderous cloud
Enwraps the sky in an ebon shroud,
    Hiding each starry ray;
While tempests howl in maniac glee,
And leaping in air, the foaming sea
    Scatters the glistening spray.

Pity the thin clad, shivering form,
That homeless wanders amid the storm,
    While ye in peace are blest;
All for want of a morsel of bread,
For lack of a place to rest the head,
    The weary limbs to rest.

Think of the features so thin and cramped,
By the demon of Penury stamped,
    The hollow cheek and eye;
Think of the children so wildly pleading,
Think of the parent that strives, unheeding,
    To list starvation's cry.

Pity the wife that dreary must watch,
A husband's dying accents to catch,
    Lone and sad must listen;

While the chattering sleet and rain
Comes dancing in through the shattered pane,
    And not one star doth glisten.

Oh, pity the eyes that seldom sleep,
That nightly a hopeless vigil keep,
    Where a mother's form doth lie;
O, weep for her that lone must yearn,
But to see the morning tapers burn,
    Within the dismal sky.

Wo! to the revelers that still rejoice,
That give no heed to Charity's voice,
    No aid of fellowship lend;
Think of the desolate, fireless hearth,
Where never is heard the voice of mirth,
    But sorrow doth ever bend.

And image the deathlike, dismal gloom
That hovers within a cheerless room,
    Where tiny form is lying;
Pity the heart in sorrow deep,
Mourn for the mother that sad must weep
    O'er famished infant dying.

Thrice blest be the poet's chainless mind,
That not even links of poverty bind—
    Penury hath not bowed;

Fame to the fetterless fancy's dreams—
That yet may fall like the sunny gleams
    Upon the worldly crowd.

Though a comfortless garret shelters him,
Though but by the rushlight burning dim,
    The golden webs are wrought;
Though passing uncheered to a pauper's grave,
O, Fame! may her gorgeous banners wave,
    Glowing with every thought!

While the ruby wine the rich man sips,
When the sparkling goblet meets his lips,
    He dreams not of sadness;
He gives no thought to the hapless poor,
While the beggar starves at his very door,
    His soul is filled with gladness.

Do we dream, 'mid the happy joys of home,
Of our soldiers brave, who daring roam
    'Mid night or stormy flood?
Who battled the traitors hand to hand;
Those who have given to save our land
    Their heart's last precious blood?

Do we sigh o'er desolate homes they left?
O'er the mother's grief of her boy bereft?
    Or the broken-hearted wife?

I fear as we crowd round the festive board,
Our thoughts too seldom wander abroad,
    To the field of death and strife.

Still, the tempest shouts in boisterous mirth,
The vexed winds scream o'er the blighted earth,
    Like merry fiends at strife;
Ye list with fear to their dismal groanings,
Yet deafly turn from sorrow's moanings,
    Amid our daily life.

Ye hark, starvation's prayer unheeding;
Yet Heaven will list affliction's pleading,
    Nor basely turn away;
And 'tis there our deeds are written down,
'Fore God's approving smile or frown,
    Till comes the reckoning day.

THE RIVAL DANCERS.

Lo! a bright scene, and 'mid the dazzling glare
Of streaming lights, glides on two beings fair,
In graceful dance, like to fabled fairy
Or charmed nymph, each moves with motion airy
In antic feats, winning the heart and eye—
With quaint agility striving still to vie

Each with the other; now they smiling meet,
With peerless gestures—while their noiseless feet
Scarce touch to earth, but ply the yielding air,
While they like winged Ideals seem floating there,
In strange unearthliness; yet what visions roll
In lava currents thro' each rival soul,
As round they whirl in sparkling, giddy maze,
Both wooing fame, both court the voice of praise,
Till the admiring throngs, in rainbow showers,
Fling at their shrine a rosy gift of flowers;
But lo! a wreath—their brows are flushed with shame,
For both have clasp'd, yet neither dare to claim;
But now their tiny feet the off'ring spurn,
And round they whirl in mazy, graceful turn;
Fair is the scene, and seeming fair each brow,
Both courting fame, and quick their life streams flow,
As now contending in mad rivalry,
They both move on 'twixt hate and jealousy.
Ah! thoughtless butterflies, an instant pause,
Nor vainly seek humanity's applause.

A SONG.

Remember me, dearest, 'mid the glory of Summer,
  When flowers are flinging their sweets on the gale;
When the lark soareth high, and the busy bee hummeth,
  And wild birds are trilling their notes in the vale.

Remember me, dearest, when the autumn wind moaneth,
  And leafless and bare, stands the old forest tree;
When the glittering sunbeams like jewels are flashing,
  And spangling the breast of the murmuring sea.

Remember me, dearest, when the winter frost cometh,
  When fairy like snowflakes are falling to earth;
When thy voice and thy heart are triumphant in gladness,
  Oh! give me a thought 'mid thy joy and thy mirth.

TO MY SISTER.

"I saw thee standing by his side,
A fair, a bright, a joyous bride."

When thou did'st breathe thy bridal vow,
  Thine eye shone with a lustre bright—
Surpassing far the lovely orbs,
  That deck the ebon brow of night.

Thou'st left the home of early days,
  Thou hast left each fond one's side—
With heart of purest innocence—
  A young and beauteous bride.

Thou'rt gone—thou'rt gone! my sister dear,
  With thy heart so free from guile;

Affection dwelt within thy breast,
　And beam'd in thy sunny smile.

A charm breathes in thy soft, sweet voice—
　Thou'rt fair as the rosy morn;
Oh! may thy path be strewn with flow'rs,
　And free from every thorn.

RAIN, DREARISOME RAIN.

I.

Rain, drearisome rain!
With sobbing, doleful strain,
Pour the shivering drops
On the bare tree-tops;
Like a living thing,
Each bubble doth spring,
　　Dripping from stem to stem.

Over mount and woods
Rain the crystal floods,
Like meteor stars
On their airy cars;
Each a fay bright world
From its orbit hurled,
　　To fell destruction doomed.

With diamond glow,
On the leafless bough
Hangs the glistening sprite,
In quivering light.
Till its tiny ball
Doth shimmer and fall,
    Shattered in sparkles bright

It should teach the heart.
To avoid a part
In the worldly glare;
For Death's sad despair
May hurry thy doom,
For amid youth's bloom—
    He slays 'mid joys of life.

II.

Rain, drearisome rain!
With sobbing, doleful strain,
Through the solemn night
Fall the drippings light,
Like sounding of feet
All my senses cheat,
    Rousing wierd fantasies.

With hurried stamp,
Like the measured tramp

Of martial hosts
Of wandering ghosts,
Pours the dismal rain
In dolorous strain,
        Seeming to patter upon my brain.

III.

Oh! the sun, the sun, the weaver sun,
A golden web for the day hath spun!
No longer the black clouds sends their springs
To deluge earth from their dripping wings;
The morn, like a jeweled queen, appears
Where the sod is gemmed with the night-rains tears;
The bladed grass through the dark ground peeps
From the secret cave where the seedling sleeps;
And soon, soon, the bride-like Spring shall come,
With her singing birds and insects' hum,
And the heart shall forget the dismal strain
That Winter sang in the dolorous rain.

CHEER EARTH'S SAD HEARTS.

Cheer Earth's sad hearts, nor hopelessly despond,
    Though Sorrow's cup your quivering lips have drain'd
Faith's balm can heal the saddest, torturing wound,
    That e'er a fainting mortal's soul hath pained;
Though false the look that once could so entrance,

Though false the words that once could so beguile,
The light of truth beams from our Saviour's glance,
  And pure affection crowns His tender smile.

Though Envy's serpent tongue would blast thy fame,
  Though whispering malice would fond hearts divide,
At last defamers shall bow low in shame,
  And plead the rocks their guilty souls to hide;
Though thou hast seen the loved by death struck down,
  And stand'st alone within this weary world,
The Sun must shine, though clouds awhile may frown,
  So yet for thee joy's bow may be unfurl'd

Though stitch by stitch thy food is earned each day,
  And hungry babes may cry to thee for bread,
Oh! pray and God will ope a brighter way,
  Ask! and it shall be given, Emmanuel said;
'Tis best like Lazarus to have suffered much,
  Nor like Dives be reckless of thy soul,
Christ still can heal, as they who once could touch
  His garments hem, found all their plagues made whole.

Then cheer sad hearts, nor sorrowing repine,
  With faith's pure shield march on through all thy cares,
Eternal joys may yet perchance be thine,
  He wins Heaven's crown who most Earth's burthens bears,
Though poverty may be your hapless fates,
  Though want shall tear the threads of life apart,
Seraphs for each shall ope the shining gates,
  And Jesus fold you to his sinless heart.

DISCORD.

Oh! never let foul discord come,
   Where love should only be;
Tho' sweet the song, one jarring note,
   Destroys the melody.
For sure where angry words are heard,
   Affection cannot dwell,
Forbearance is the holy charm,
   Such evil pow'r to quell.

And mortal's discord should not come
   Where heart is bound to heart;
Ah! know where Satan's shafts are hurl'd,
   Love's link may rend apart.
For where dissension comes between,
   It breaks true sympathy,
As 'mid contending elements
   Exists no harmony.

Let not mischievous demon's pow'r,
   The heart's stern passions move,
Home is the place where gentleness
   Should rule with perfect love.
See how God's universe moves on,
   In unity divine,
And by his nobler plan direct,
   That little sphere of thine.

POWER OF HOPE.

Life without hope—oh! 'twere a cheerless way,
   A desert vast, whereon no fount may spring,
For e'en as sunbeam gilds the light of day,
   So hope o'er life her radiant bow doth fling.

The mother fond, sends forth her cherished son,
   To meet and combat with all worldly ill,
In fancy oft she views hope's summit won,
   And visions bright her doting bosom fill.

The lover parteth from the gentle maid,
   Smiling with hope, she his faith believing,
Admits no doubt the ideal form to shade
   Within her soul—no thought of earth's deceiving.

In sombre room, 'mid penury and woe,
   A being lies in poverty's extreme,
Starving, and ill, yet what sustains life's flow,
   Within that form?—'tis hope's exulting beam.

The wife marks him to whom her vow was giv'n,
   Wasting existence for inebriate's grave;
Yet 'mid her griefs she pleading looks to heav'n,
   Trusting to hope, that God, that God will save.

Without thee, oh! the heart might never bear
  With life's vexations, 'twere a darksome way,
Bleak as a starless night, for 'mid our care,
  'Tis hope sustains us with her quenchless ray.

LOVE ME WHILE I'M HERE.

When I am dead weep not in gloom,
  Above my lowly bier,
Ah! mourn me not when in the tomb,
  But love me while I'm here.

When sorrow's gloom is on my brow.
  Let love be nigh to cheer;
While yet on earth oh prize me now,
  Yes, love me while I'm here.

What comfort bring ye to the dead
  By mournful sigh or tear?
For me I'd rather tears were shed,
  When woes shall meet me here.

Though I the lost may fondly prize,
  And mourn them sad and drear,
I ask no pangs when closed mine eyes,
  But love me while I'm here.

Oh! give me kindly words of truth,
  When sorrows hover near;
Ah! weep me not when cold in death,
  But love me while I'm here.

THE LITTLE ANGEL.

'Twas when the golden summer bloom'd,
  When swift the shining moments pass,
And bright the clustering roses gleam'd,
  And smiled the daisy in the grass;
Seem'd there an angel in our midst,
  With cherub face and ringlets bright,
But God has ta'en our heavenly gift,
  Up to his home in endless light!

No more we'll hear that infant voice,
  In sweetness lisp and mimic word,
No more we'll hear the baby laugh,
  Soft as the song of summer bird;
No more we'll mark the red lips part,
  And gleam the tiny pearly teeth,
No more the ivory lids unfold,
  And show the heav'n-hued eyes beneath.

'Ere yet the sturdy Autumn came,
  And harvest yet had reap'd her store,
Our bright one sought that better world,
  Where summer's bloom is never o'er;
Scarce had we dreamed how dear thou wert,
  How fond we loved thee and how true,
Till death had hid thy tiny form,
  Forever from our longing view.

Now stalwart winter robes the earth,
  With snowy wreath and gems of frost,
And mem'ry wand'ring o'er the past,
  In anguish weeps the loved and lost;
Ceased the fond mother now to clasp
  Her sinless infant to her breast;
But there's a balm to soothe her woe,
  We know that thou art with the blest.

NEVER PUT OFF TILL TO-MORROW.

Ah! never put off 'till to-morrow
  What God has assigned for to-day;
Meet life's cares each moment is bringing—
  You'll find 'tis the easiest way.

Your duties, why seek to avoid them?
    Putting off, putting off all you can;
Face evils at once that assail you—
    You'll find 'tis the happiest plan,

Your sick neighbor sighs for your coming,
    But pleasures allure you to-day;
Perchance you will seek him to-morrow,
    And meet but the spiritless clay.

While you can, to homeless and starving,
    Of your comforts, give but your mite;
For the angels in heaven are waiting,
    Each moment your good deeds to write.

Let plans of God's Universe teach you
    How each law His will doth obey;
Could night's darkness wait 'till to-morrow,
    And gloom on the beams of the day?

Could seasons the work heav'n appoints them.
    Put off even moments or hours?
Could Summer—her task getting weary—
    Wait for Autumn to blossom her flow'rs?

Yet we mortals with thoughtless presumption,
    Shrink from duties each day should be borne;
Aye! waiting to-morrow to do them,
    That, here, for us never may dawn.

MY HEART'S PRAYER.

Father of mercy! God, in pity guide
  My heart in virtue, truth and holy love,
Keep me from that bright path, so fair and wide,
  Teach me the narrow way that leads above;
All selfish feelings cast from out my heart,
  My mind from every earthly dreaming win,
Teach me, oh Lord, to love the better part,
  Nor bow my soul in servitude to sin.

Fom our wrung hearts, the loving and the true,
  But late stern death has laid within the tomb,
Heaven's glories burst upon his spirit's view,
  While we bow down in agonizing gloom;
My God! my God, 'tis hard to part with those,
  We e'en have cherished as an angel guest,
To know the kindly eyes for aye must close
  E'en though we feel that they are surely blest.

The quivering lips in struggling anguish cry,
  Thy will be done—knowing that will is just,
Yet oh, I'd rather lie me down and die,
  Than have a loved form laid within the dust.
Fain would I that my spirit wings were furl'd,
  And I with him who came man's soul to save,
If I were fitted for that better world,
  Fain would I fly beyond the silent grave.

Perhaps Thy will is, I on earth must stay.
  For one who yet must linger sadly on;
To chase the shadows from her troubled way,
  Until, my mother, thou thy crown hast won,
Then teach me, Lord, to follow him on earth,
  My angel brother—inspire my mortal breast,
With all the virtues that made up his worth,
  To make those happy whom his presence blest.

Not for himself he lived, but those he loved,
  No selfish passions swayed his act or word,
With kindly motives every heart-beat moved,
  E'en like Bethsada as by angels stirred,
Savior, like him, oh let me truly be,
  Not for myself to feel, but others woe,
Until the gates of death shall ope for me,
  And I with joy our loved one's weal shall know.

LOOKING INTO EYES THAT LOVE US.

When looking into eyes that love us,
  And seeing there our image gleam,
While the glorious stars above us,
  Watch their faces in the stream;
Listening vows of tender plighting,
  And never doubting of their truth,

Not a thought of care, or blighting,
  Oh! thus the dreamy light of youth!

Ah! could it only last forever,
  Would hearts were faithful as they seem,
That cruel change might never—never,
  Make clouds where sunshine us'd to gleam;
Would mortals aye might trust each other,
  Nor malice sever friendship's tie,
But each like sister, and like brother,
  On true affection e'er rely.

Would we might look in eyes that love us,
  Nor ever fear their faithless glow,
Would no foreboding thought might move us,
  To doubt the hearts we seem to know!
Would love might never feel a blighting,
  That all were faithful as they seem.
That vows might never cease their plighting,
  Nor time e'er blast youth's happy dream.

DREAM NOT OF CLOUDS WHEN SUNBEAMS SHINE.

Warn me not the love I cherish,
  May, like the sunlight, pass away,
Say not e'er affections perish,

E'en like the fading light of day,
Rather bid glad fancy whisper,
  Of fairer scenes, of happier hours,
Let new born hope, the cheerful lisper,
  Paint life of wreathing beams and flowers.

If ills come, we e'en must meet them;
  But let the present hour of joy,
With no forebodings wait to greet them,
  And every peaceful thought destroy;
'Tis time enough to bow and languish,
  When stern grief wakes thy soul's unrest,
Oh! think, the spectre of pale anguish,
  Her draught to Jesus' lips hath prest.

And strive with all thy mortal weakness,
  Whatever woes thy steps betide,
To imitate our Saviour's meekness,
  When the sharp spear had rent his side;
But if the present's filled with gladness,
  Be thankful that such peace is thine,
Nor paint the future cloth'd in sadness,
  Dream not of clouds when sunbeams shine.

JUDGE NOT, LEST YE BE JUDGED.

Why forever seem we chiding,
　Our hapless neighbors for their lacks,
'Twere better all their failings hiding,
　Than heaping burthens on their backs.

Just look at home with fear and trembling,
　Are all but virtues there we see ?
Know with God there's no dissembling,
　He can see both you and me.

Why a generous action scouting ?
　Thinking all a mere pretension;
Why every kindly feeling doubting ?
　Mocking at a good intention.

Our own good deeds forever vaunting,
　Doth not bespeak a righteous heart,
'Tis not by sneering gibes and taunting,
　True virtue acts her angel part.

If in strong, delusive blindness.
　Some thoughtless creature turns astray,
Then let us with true meaning kindness,
　Point them again the better way.

'Twere best if each ourselves preparing,
   To fight 'gainst Satan's dark assaults,
Than in jeering wonder staring,
   At some stumbling mortals faults.

If we at home would look with keenness,
   And let our neighbors' failings rest,
We need not further search for meanness,
   Than in our frail and jeering breast.

A view of self might make a little
   Kinder judgment of our brother,
And we might cease, perchance, to whittle,
   Characters for one another.

JEALOUSY.

Lo! the green monster sports at Linda's heart,
Gleams in her smile and in her glances dart,
Tho' at her shrine proud suitors bend the knee,
She loves but one, the chosen Manfredie;
While at another's feet she views him kneeling,
And with the agony of slighted feeling,
Transfixed she stands as crazed with thoughts intense,
'Twas thus he wooed her but an instant thence.

And does he seek to win another now—
Would he thus perjure his late plighted vow?
His heart so soon, oh! could it seek to rove—
Dare he thus tamper with a woman's love?
Her pulses leap, her eyes grow wildly bright,
And her flushed cheeks now turn to ashey white;
She tears the bright wreath from her pallid brow,
His fingers wove and flings it from her now
In very scorn, viewing each withered leaf
So late in bloom, fit emblem of her grief;
Now vents her anguish in a flood of tears,
While her wrung heart is madly racked with fears,
As the fierce battling of the winds and wave,
E'en so her thoughts in quick confusion rave.

"Yet does she hate him ?"—nay, but she the fair,
That heedless won him in her simple snare;
(Too apt we are the guiltless one to blame
And brand the innocent with other's shame).
Reversed the scene, and lo! amid the dance
Fair Linda glides; her eyes shoot forth a glance
Of happy triumph, as stately by her side,
A proud form moves with all a lover's pride—

"But where is Manfredie"—apart he stands
With heaving breast and wildly clasping hands,
Now pressing tightly on his forehead bare,
As if to still the thoughts that struggle there

In hurried strife, his pale lips part
As 'twere to speak, but no sound doth start
The voiceless air, while his o'er burdened brain
Whirls in delirium, every nerve doth strain
In quick convulsions, while o'er his soul,
Fancies like fire-winged meteors roll;
All other sound, all other sense is lost
In this one sorrow—every feeling's tost
And mangled in the embittered fray.

Yet does he love her?—yes, as sun to day,
His heart still clings, his idol's still divine,
Tho'round his brain mad thoughts like serpents twine.
But lo! his rival at his feet lies bleeding,
Oh! *jealousy, thou vip'rous reptile feeding*
On *human hearts*, how fearful is thy power!
Insat'ate fiend, 'for thee the mightiest cower.
Oh! Earth's deluded, know ye his demon art
That wakes such feelings in the mortal heart?

A LIFE SKETCH.

Happy we wander'd on that beaut'ous shore,
　Where 'twas our wont in childhood's hours to roam,
Joyous we listen'd to proud ocean's roar
　Around that spot, our lovely sea-girt home;

Thou wert a dreaming child, scarce in thy teens,
  And I yet blushing to that time so fraught
With hope, when many a jewel rich fancy gleans
  From out the poet's treasury of thought;
And mirth and gladness laugh'd in thy bright eye,
  While rosy tinges flush'd thy downy cheek.

To the calm past we gave no ling'ring sigh.
  Ours was that peace the tongue might fail to speak,
So exquisite our happiness seem'd there,
  All things around were fill'd with mirth and joy;
Our hearts knew not the voice of dark despair,
  No grief—no ill the soul would e'er annoy.
Yet oft at sorrow's tale the trembling tear
  Of sympathy into the eye would start,
But scarce we dream'd that grief could linger here,
  Each deeming the world was like her own young heart.

But change and death brought griefs on which to dwell
  In thoughtful hours, tho' crowding years forsooth,
And we awaken'd from the holy spell.
  The blissful dream that lit our childish youth,
And we had wander'd from that sweet retreat
  Unto a place less lovely, where no flow'r
Breath'd on the summer air its perfume sweet,
  And strange and weary seem'd each passing hour,
Thy cheeks were pale—care dimm'd thy beaming eye,
  While the sad tear of sorrow oft would flow,

And from thy breast would burst the heavy sigh,
  Which told of grief, the pangs of sudden woe.

But there came change—the mightiest change of all,
  And we were mingling in the worldly crowd;
Gaily we glided through the festive hall,
  Where music's voice rang merrily and loud,
And we were far from that delightful shore,
  And from the warble of our rippling stream,
To look on them—we thought, oh! never more,
  To see reflected there the starlight gleam!

Yet we were gay, though in the world, apart
  From all its worldliness, we seem'd as one;
Scarce thought arose in either youthful heart,
  The other knew not; and so time roll'd on.
And suitors came and went, and came again,
  Yet still united walked we on thro' life;
It seem'd a mystic and a mighty chain
  Had linked our souls with sweet affection rife.

Ambition oped for thee her gilded arms,
  And Fame's loud trumpet in proud triumph rang,
Yet neither lur'd thee with their thousand charms;
  In vain to thee their wizard voices sang,
The patriot, statesman, noblest of the land,
  In homage wooed; proud hearts bow'd low to thee;
It seem'd some nymph had waved her mystic wand,
  And clothed thee with a spell of witchery.

Yet thou, unconscious of thy winning power,
  In duty's path to walk dost simply try,
As all so innocent the fairest flow'r,
  In adoration chains the gazer's eye.
Though lauding crowds proclaim'd thy mind's great
      worth,
  And many came to win thy gentle heart,
Yet thou could'st turn from all the praise of earth,
  In humble faith to act thy mortal part.

Loving and kind in ev'ry deed and word,
  Ah! blessed heart that claims thy truthful love,
Thou gifted one; heaven alone has stirr'd
  Thy pow'r of genius; nought but God could move,
And wake an earthly lyre with strain like thine,
  And though so shrinking from the blaze of fame,
Yet she for thee her crowning wreath shall twine,
  And sing to nations thy immortal name.

What next shall change? for thou and I no more
  Watch the glad sunlight gild our favorite stream;
With those beloved we dwell far from that shore;
  Sister, at most life's but a changing dream.

SONG.

I love thee still, I love thee still,
   As in those faded hours,
When fancies elves their glories wove,
   Of sunny beams and flowers;
I love thee, tho, thine eyes are dim,
   Tho' cheek and lips have faded,
To me there's beauty on thy brow,
   By trace of grief o'er shaded.

I love thee still, I love the still,
   As in those days departed,
'Ere sorrow left thee stricken thus
   Bereft and broken hearted;
I love thee still—and as to earth,
   Returns the morning's beaming,
So thoughts in rapture clings to thee,
   Like star in mem'ry gleaming.

SING FOR THE BOWL.

Sing for the bowl, the sparkling bowl,
   As it glowing meets the lips,
Sing 'tis death to the human soul,
   And a curse to him who sips.

Ah! fly from one who loves the gleam,
  Of the red wine's shining glance,
Though thou'rt charm'd by love's happy dream,
  Break, break from its blissful trance.

Maiden fair with the crimson cheeks,
  And sorrowless, hopeful heart,
Turn from the flattering words he speaks,
  For Oh! each is Satan's dart.

Though he kneels, a suppliant, at thy feet,
  Oh! heed not his fervent vow;
He finds the ruby wine more sweet
  Than a kiss from that snowy brow.

Beware his glance, its burning glow,
  May thy gentle bosom win,
Fly from its spell ere waked to know,
  That a demon hides within.

Thou joyous bride, the flowers that now,
  Are wreathing thy lovely head,
'Twere better they had decked thy brow,
  Among the glorious dead.

Weary watcher through night so drear,
  Thou may'st pine in sorrow gaunt,
While thy restless babe, is nestling near,
  Moaning in pitiful want.

Thou of a broken heart may'st tell,
  But a wreck of mad despair,
Where once but smiles of joy would dwell,
  Of a brow now seam'd with care.

Sing then, the bowl, the sparkling bowl!
  As it, glowing, meets the lips,
Sing 'tis death to the human soul,
  And a curse to him who sips.

WHY DID YE GANG AWA.

Willie why did ye gang awa
  Frae ane who dearly lo'ed ye?
Sin' then mony a laddie braw,
  Has fondly sought and wooed me;
But still my puir heart sighs and pines;
  For oh! it lo'ed thee mickle,
An' still luv's spell my bosom twines,
  For ane sae fause an fickle.

Come back as in the days gane by.
  An' to your breast enfold me,
Come breath again wi' gentle sigh,
  Sweet vows as ance ye told me;

In vain my dotin' heart may plead,
  In vain my tears an' sighin',
Ye wadna to my cry tak heed,
  Though Nellie's sel' were dyin'.

OUR COUNTRY.

All mournfully like solemn dirge.
  Throughout our land is sent;
The widow and the orphan's wail;
  The mother's sad lament.

See Liberty with ghastly mien,
  With precious life blood stained;
Of martyrs who to save her fall,
  Their hearts' last drop have drained.

Antietam on thy ghastly field.
  The moon's sad gleamings shed,
Where dying men in helpless woe,
  Lay heaped among the dead.

'Twere well if then our mother earth,
  Had ope'd her gory breast,
And in her heart each pain racked soul,
  Had folded into rest.

Crush this rebellion, freedom's sons,
  Thrust down each traitor knave,
And from disunion's fearful curse;
  Our lovely country save.

At Gettysburg we drove them back
  Like chaff by wild winds blown;
Oh! braver men than our's were there,
  The world has never known.

Through every State the tocsin rings,
  Of bloody war's alarms;
The soldier clasps his weeping wife,
  Within his sturdy arms;

His country calls and they must part,
  No more perchance to meet,
Until the angel Death shall bear,
  Each to the Savior's feet.

Lo! *PORTER the brave hero boy,
  Last of that gallant band,
So dauntlessly he met the foe,
  All proudly did he stand;

---

*At the Battle of Roanoke Island, when all his men had fallen around him, Benjamin F. Porter stood bravely to his guns, dauntlessly loading and discharging, and alone nobly defended his position against the rebels until relieved by Hawkin's Zouaves.

The rest had fallen 'mid shell and shot,
  And yet that fearless son,
The battle faced triumphantly,
  Till victory was won.

Tears, heart-rung tears, in lava floods,
  In thousand homes are shed;
Above the loved in battle slain,
  Columbia's patriot dead:

A Lyon, Baker, Ellsworth too,
  Who died our flag to save;
And every noble volunteer,
  That fills a soldier's grave.

Though Vicksburg cost us many a life,
  Ere yet the siege was done;
Thousands of prisoners crowned our arms,
  When we the field had won;

And Sumpter she shall yet be ours,
  Though mighty be the fray;
Our shell, like heaven-sent thunderbolts,
  Shall rend her walls away.

Our Banks, our Butler, Burnside, Grant,
  Have led their valiant men,
And met base treason in his hold,
  Like lion in his den.

Hungry and weary they have rushed,
　To battle with the foe
On many a field—and proudly oft
　They've struck the conqueror's blow.

Mangled and maimed, fathers and sons,
　Lie on their pallets low,
While some in maniac frenzy rave,
　'Mid fever's quenchless glow;

In vain the dying soldier mourns,
　To grasp some friendly hand;
The fainting breath, the glazing eye,
　Then stills life's ebbing sand.

Oh, Liberty! what tears; what blood,
　Hath dimmed thy precious ray!
How could fell traitors meanly dare
　Sweet freedom to betray ?

When like the sun shall thy blessed beams
　Shine through our stricken land ?
And States in peaceful bonds unite.
　As friends clasp hand with hand.

Our country wails her noblest sons,
　Slain 'mid the fearful strife;
Where brother sends the knelling shot,
　That stills a brother's life;

How long, how long, our people moan,
  Shall this sad havoc be?
Oh, God? a weeping nation cries
  For succor unto thee.

THE VALLEY OF MARIPOSA.

My valley home, my heart with rapture thrills,
As gazing now on thy majestic hills,
While high to heav'n each holds his noble crest,
In fading hues of dying verdure drest,
Each proudly wears his coronet of trees,
Tossing their leaflets in the dancing breeze;
But down their jagged sides the beamy rill
Hath no glad song of laughing joy to trill,
And on the wild flow'r in her grassy nest.
The burning Sol his parting kiss hath prest.
Here boasting pride doth no proud mansion raise,
Whose painted windows flaunt the sunny blaze,
With frescoed hills, and high uprearing dome,
As yet in thee, the modest cottage home,
The peasant's choice hath sheltered poor and great,
As if all generous here the God of Fate
His kindly gifts more equally had spread,
As day's glad beams alike to all are shed.
Tho' once 'mid proudest magnates of our land,

My way hath been—the true, the tender hand
Of fond affection would I far more prize,
Than tinsel'd wealth, with feeings's sacrifice;
Where faith and love are cast away for show,
That soon may pass e'en like the melting snow,
To leave us wrecked and 'lorn till we again
Rouse up to know that earthly pomp is vain.
Ah, sure contentment here might peaceful rest,
Nor fear the stab of envy in her breast.
How fair thy vales for sighing swain to rove,
With her the chosen Hebe of his love,
While Luna wreaths with light the griefless way,
Where they in love's enchanted moments stray;
Oh, many a pleasing tale with myst'ry rife,
Thy rocks could tell of the wild Indian's life,
Of maid and chief, and warriors bold and brave,
That now have past on time's destroying wave.
Fair Mariposa—nature's sweet retreat,
Far from the hum of cities' busy feet,
Girded by mounts whose summits tow'ring high,
Like giant wraiths stand 'gainst the twilight sky;
Thy wond'rous charms my dreaming soul inspire,
To wake for thee my long neglected lyre;
Once more I clasp the loved of childhood's day
As was my wont—my joyful children play
At grandpa's knee—oh! happiness complete,
The peaceful hearth where the home faces meet.
Here Summer as a happy infant wakes,

And o'er the hills her sunny tresses shakes,
While Flora from her rosy fingers show'rs
Her jeweled wreaths of fairy rainbow flow'rs;
Pomona lovely, in her regal charms,
The varied fruits bears in her rounded arms,
While ripening grapes her shining girdle twine,
And in the sunbeams like bright rubies shine.
But fading Autumn comes with churlish mien
To blast the flow'rs and fade the leaflets green,
The rose's heart touched by his frosty breath,
Helpless expires in sudden throes of death;
Winter his angry draught of storms doth quaff,
Rude winds shall howl as if the demon's laugh
Had echoed from the dark myster'ous bow'rs
Of imp and fiend, in this glad world of our's,
And rains o'er dingle, dale, and dark isl'd woods,
In gleaming shafts shall pour their dashing floods.
But blithesome Spring like some coquettish maid,
Must come again and dance o'er hill and glade,
And wheresoe'er her fay-like footsteps pass,
Shall spring the clover and the daisied grass;
I love thy vales, I love thy balmy breeze,
That fan my cheek—far, far across the seas
I left my home, to seek for health in thee,
And thou hast proved new life, indeed, to me.

THE WINTER WINDS.

Chill, chill and cold, blows the winter winds,
   Thro' nook and crevice cramping;
Over the hill, and over the vale,
   Like battling Furies tramping.

Who smiles to greet ye! oh! who may hail?
   Who joys to meet ye again?
Penury's nurslings, poverty's brood
   Can they bless your cheerless reign.

With ye comes sorrow, sickness, and pain,
   With ye comes want and weeping;
The shelterless form, the pauper's death,
   The heart with terror heaping.

What tho' with draping so pearly white,
   The trees so gorgeous dressing;
Who gladdens to meet ye—frosty elves,
   Who hails your bleak caressing.

Come, cease the tones o'er the blasted earth,
   Of your wild and boist'rous singing,
For ever to ye the trio grim;
   Death, Woe, and Want, are clinging.

To thee, oh! God, 'mid every ill,
  The faithful heart is turning!
For thou art the lowly being's friend,
  Whom the thoughtless world is spurning.

MOCK ME NOT WITH FLATT'RING WILES.

Nay, mock me not with flatt'ring wiles,
  Be honest, candid, just,
I love to list to truthful words
  I fearlessly may trust;
The welcome smile, the kindly glance,
  The guileless manly speech,
I love them—fashion's studied arts,
  My heart may never reach.

Nay, woo me not with flatt'ring words,
  For me they have no spell.
But all thy heart's true sentiments,
  In homely phrases tell;
I would not hear vain praises sang,
  'Till I would almost dream,
Myself the ideal, fancied nymph,
  Thou fain would'st make me seem.

MY MOTHER.

My sainted mother—gone from earth and me,
   My soul in agony laments thy loss,
Like the mad swelling of the stormy sea,
   When the wild waves in hurried frenzy toss;
      So felt my heart when gazing on thy face,
      Where Death, the victor, left his whiten'd trace.

With angel patience thou didst calmly bear
   The racking pangs that pierced thy faded form,
Still trusting meekly to our Savior's care,
   To take the safely thro' death's rending storm;
      And thou hast past into heaven's endless rest,
      To lean in peace on Jesus' tender breast.

Oh! mother—mother—my heart's highest love,
   Thou idol, treasur'd dearer far than life,
And can'st thou now from that bright home above,
   Look on thine own amid earth's scenes of strife?
      Do'st thou, dear mother, fond and earnest pray
      That we shall meet thee in eternal day?

My God! my God! rings on my throbbing brain,
   The words thy cherished lips had uttered last,
'Ere as convulsed by some destroying pain,
   Thy gentle spirit had forever past;
      Thine earnest eyes seem gazing on me now,
      While my heart writhes in agonizing wo.

So linked—so knit—my being was with thine,
  My soul with thee seem'd struggling forth to go.
But thou hast passed—and we in anguish pine
  'Neath the sad tortures of Fate's keenest blow;
    But Faith still whispers 'mid care's blighting pain,
    That we shall meet thee, mother—meet again.

And thou hast left me—kind and loving hearts,
  Who hold with me thy very mem'ry dear,
And, hand in hand, we'll strive to do our parts
  In Christian deeds—until those waters clear
    Of never-ending life burst on our sight,
    And we behold thee there a seraph bright.

FANCY AND LOVE.

Oh what is love the Poets theme,
A gilded toy—a passing dream,
A silken cord to gently bend
Together kindred heart, and mind,
A breath of air—a fleeting sigh,
A Meteor in the summer sky,
Thus false hearts deem loves truth will pall,
As fancy's Castles fade and fall.
The perfume exhaled by a flow'r,

That blooms, and dies, within an hour;
On thee no lasting seal is set,
Thou'rt here—thou'rt gone—and they forget,
A dream forgotten when past by,
A rainbow in a stormy sky,
A Lute's tone borne upon the wind,
That leaves no memory behind.
A charm that fades like mist away,
A snow-flake in the blaze of day;
A bright, a gorgeous butterfly,
That with the roses breath must die;
A spell that doth as quickly pass,
As beauty mirror'd in the glass.
The soft sweet tone—the bright eyes glance,
All fade when waking from this trance,
All fade—nor e'er return again,
As flitting cloud, or April rain;
A spell the heart's surface shading,
Like moonbeams from the waters fading.
A Silver Lake whereon doth beam,
The first, and last of starlights' gleam,
But which when dark clouds o'er it low'r,
Doth lose its bright reflecting pow'r,
Thus love they say thy dreamings end,
When shadows with thy sunlight blend.
Thus groveling Nature's dream loves art,
The POWER that STIRS the FAITHLESS HEART,
And ever nurse the wierd deceit,
Of Elfish fancy, FICKLE CHEAT,

And call it LOVE'S ETERNAL POW'R—
That bee-like flits from flow'r to flow'r.
From fair, to fair, they changing roam,
Nor seek the sweet content of home;
Choosing from all the world beside,
A true, a faithful, loving bride;
THE EDEN PICTURE OF OUR EARTH,
TWO CONSTANT HEARTS BESIDE ONE HEARTH.
That is not Love, the fickle wight,
That like Chameleon with the light,
Changes for aye from hue to hue,
But fancy—faithless and untrue,
Love—Essence from the pow'r above,
Thou gift divine for God is love!

◆

PEAN FOR LIBERTY

America I sing of thee,
"Thou land of freedom and the free,
Home of the Sons of Liberty.
Long with the records of thy fame,
Shall blend our country's patriots' name,
Not he—like stern Napoleon,
For glory of an earthly throne,
And fame that false ambition yields,

For self—would wade through gory fields,
But struck to succor and to save,
Our Washington—the nobly brave.
That name shall ring from age to age
And thrill the hero and the sage;
While nations hail from ev'ry strand,
The soil where Freedom waved her brand!
As Jove's voice sounding through the sky.
When mount and rock in turn reply:
As streams the sunlight from on high;
So all earth yet her seas shall lave,
While thrones sink down beneath the wave,
And monarchies and kingdoms fall,
Like meteors from night's starry wall.
Well may the eagle soar on high,
And dart into the beaming sky,
The emblem of our liberty.
A curse is on our lovely land,
For martyrs' blood hath stained the hand
Of her white men—the butchered slaves,
That cry from their forgotten graves,
Who perished 'neath the lash's wounds,
Or torn to death by murderous hounds.
My God! was it before thine eyes,
Fort Pillow's fiendish sacrifice?
Or did'st thou turn aside and pause,
Till these slave men for freedom's cause,
Had given as offering their poor lives,
Which thou, just God, wilt not despise:

Does it seem just, and right, and wise,
That blood must wash away the stain,
Left on our land by slavery's chain ?
Nailed to the cross like thy dear Son,
Did'st mark them there each quivering one,
Then thrust in graves ere life was done,*
Sure each, heaven's brightest crown hath won,
To link thy States fair sisterhood,
Brave men have given their heart's best blood,
A fearful, yet a precious flood.
Where freedom laves her fest'ring hands,
Still bound by slavery's rotting bands,
But soon shall rend the cank'ring chain;
For like Atlantics stormy main,
The armies meet like battling waves,
'Fore our brave men those traitor knaves
Must flee—or like mean dastards die,
And fill foul graves of infamy.
Treason doth thy escutcheon stain,
But soon must end her sanguine reign,
With breaking of the bondsman's chain.
Though factions striving to divide,
Cast justice, equal rights aside,
Trampling Libertas to the earth,
Like Phœnix, she'll renew her birth!

*When the Southerners captured Fort Pillow, they crucified the
negroes, and taking them from the crosses while yet alive, buried
them.

Still, still united thou shalt be.
And mock the demon knavery;
Inviting now, but foulest heart,
To tear thy struggling limbs apart,
Thy glorious States—the social chain,
That binds them in a sister train,
What fiend would rend the link in twain ?
Columbia—my native shore,
Thy very sunlight I adore;
Long may thy vessels plow the seas,
And spread their canvass to the breeze,
And heaven defend the gallant tars
That man them 'neath thy stripes and stars.
Still commerce pour from ev'ry land,
And fling her treasures on thy strand;
While there's a voice, thy praise be sung,
And shouted on from tongue to tongue.
Thou land of freedom and the free,
I join the song of liberty,
My loved America, for thee.

TRUST ON.

" 'Tis each one for himself, and our God for us all,"
  A motto that governs our world in a measure,
Tho' with semblance of friendship some fondly may greet,
  Too oft 'tis you add to their gain, or their pleasure ;

Yet brave hearts there are.   Yes the candid and true,
  But 'tis not at the feast, or revel they're nigh;
And in moments of grief when sorrows beset us,
  That the voice of *pure sympathy* hushes the sigh.

Let not mistrust like a spectre e'er haunt you,
  Tho' thy faith were betrayed and confidence shaken,
Gild the future with hope, for *all* are not *false.*
  Still trust though *reality* bids you awaken;
If soft words of kindness and gentleness bless you.
  Never doubt—for in truth and affection believing;
'Tis happier far than to live in suspicion,
  Still to BLINDLY TRUST ON tho' all were deceiving.

LINES TO JEAN.

Though each act and word be cherish'd,
  So fondly now beloved by thee,
If, perchance, this form had perished,
  How soon it might forgotten be!

I have seen the prized—late lying
  In her mouldering earthly bed;
I have watched dear mem'ries dying.
  Swift as withered leaves are shed.

When for aye these eyes are closing,
  Thou may'st sigh with sad regret,
But 'ere long in death reposing,
  Thou might'st too, beloved forget.

Forgot—forgot—alone—forsaken,
  By those who look and word would prize,
Oh! say at times my mem'ry 'll awaken,
  And mirth give way to weary sighs.

Not that I would thou should'st languish,
  If heaven should sever heart from heart,
O'er fates' decrees ne'er bend in anguish,
  Bear on, whate'er thy earthly part;

But oh! not for this world's gay pleasure,
  Cast my lone image from thy soul;
There let it live—a simple treasure,
  'Till life's last sadden'd chime shall toll.

⸻⸺◆⸺ ⸻

THE WIFE'S DEVOTION.

Forget thee? no! by all the heart wrung tears,
For thee I've wept, by the long trust of years,
By the bless'd vow that knit our hearts in one,
Thou know'st I love, thou seem'st to me a sun

To light my way, and love, oh! love, hast thou
Forgot that hour, when, by our mutual vow
By angels sealed, though made on mortal earth,
Each swore to love thro' care, thro' joy and mirth?

Forget thee? no! until in death I sleep,
I'll trust in love, still, still my heart shall keep
Its pledge to thee, tho' sorrow's chilling blight
Should kill my peace, and life seem one long night!
I'll love thee still, tho' time and seasons range,
Within my heart thou ne'er shalt trace a change!
Full well thou know'st whatever my fate may be,
Thou'lt ever be as dear as now to me!

THE SOLDIER'S DYING WIFE.

Fold me closer, I am dying,
   Heavenly anthems greet mine ears,
Oh! I hear the angel minstrels
   Chant the music of the spheres;
On the fearful field of battle,
   Where Death's missiles pour'd like rain,
My husband, my beloved one,
   Lay bleeding 'mong the slain.

They wrapt him in the Stars and Stripes,
　　Wet with his drops of life—
Shall he not come a spirit bright,
　　To meet his dying wife?
Fain would I watch that clay cold form,
　　As Juana* once so vain,
Waited for heaven to give her back
　　Her chosen knight again.

I have loved thee well, my country,
　　And bade my dear one go,
And for thy rights and Liberty,
　　To battle with the foe.
I sacrificed mine earthly peace
　　At Freedom's storm-beat shrine,
And now for thee I offer up
　　This broken heart of mine.

Ah! I have pined for weary days,
　　But Life's cords gave way at last;
I'll hail the hour when this worn soul
　　From weary earth has passed.
My tiny babe, with seraph mien,

---

* Juana, mother of the Emperor Charles the V, upon the death of her husband, Phillip the Handsome, of Austria, had his body laid in state, magnificently dressed, and watched over it in the hope of returning life, until from its state of decomposition she could endure it no longer.

Smiles in estatic joy;
  Grim Death, hold back thy fatal spell,
    And spare me to my boy !

Fold me closer, I am dying,
  Colder grows my gasping breath;
Fold me closer, oh! my mother,
  For I feel the chill of Death.
Faint and fainter comes each whisper,
  Sad the weary eyelids close;
Slowly ebb life's surging ripples
  To Death's quieting repose.

DAWN.

Lovely she wakes as from Elysian bow'rs,
  Some goddess fair dawned on our mortal sight;
Lovely she wakes as on a throne of flow'rs,
  Celestial form in glory's robes bedight;
O'er nature's quiet in full grandeur breaking,
The eastern skies in floods of brightness laking.

While like a vanquished Queen the dim night yieldeth,
  Till the last star withdraws its timid glances;
And morn the victors sceptre proudly wieldeth,
  As on triumphal car she slow advances;

The earth and, air with roseate hues caressing,
Seeming to breathe o'er all a whispered blessing.

The sparkling beauty of her light distilling,
  O'er all the world in floods of amber streaming,
The void of space with flames of glory filling,
  While in the East the gorgeous clouds are gleaming;
As 't were forgiving heav'ns resplendent portals,
Inviting ope'd to us repentant mortals.

Seeming to bear to all a holy greeting,
  From the immortal, the ethereal band;
The thoughtful skies in robes of splendor sheeting,
  As 'twere reflections from that better land;
Our truant hearts from this dark earth to win
Unto that world where never entereth sin.

The Tyrian dyes like Seraph wings outspreading,
  O'er the deep quiet of the heavenly plain;
Now far and near their changeful glances shedding,
  And pouring to earth like gems of golden rain;
Till the dazzling Monarch of the day ascends,
And with her light his fiery shafting blends.

THE MOTHER'S WATCH.

O'er her daughter's form a mother wept,
   Where hover'd the spectre of death;
And her sad heart throbbed in sorrow deep,
   As she listen'd the fainting breath;
      That went and came,
      Through the heaving frame,
   With quick convulsive rushing;
      In hurried flow,
      Quiver and thro',
   The tide of life was gushing.

Eve's hour had past, and the midnight dawn'd,
   Yet the " Vital Spark" remained;
But more feebly and ever fainter,
   Life's flickering taper waned,
      With sorrow wild,
      Above her child.
   She prayed for morning's light;
      There sad weeping,
      And lone keeping,
   Her drear vigil thro' the night.

And yet, she dreamed of life and health,
   'Aye the truant hope believing;
Still fancy pictured years to come,
   The mother's heart deceiving.

And in her breast,
Grief sank to rest,
And joy its radiance shed,
But e'er dawning,
Of the morning,
The vision bright had fled.

And bowed in agony of soul,
Oh! she mourned in anguish there;
While myriad hearts rejoiced in mirth,
Her's withered in wild despair.
As hast'ning by,
The moments fly,
And joined the shrouded past;
Oh! yet seeming,
As but dreaming,
Lo! the angel spirit past.

THE SUICIDE.

The cypress-like guardian spirits wave,
O'er the silent turf of a lowly grave;
There bright birds of summer sweetly sing,
There violet and primrose together spring,
Yet no tablet stands forth in boasting fame,
No record is there of a cherish'd name;

But the sunbeams like warning spectres glide
O'er the grave of a hapless suicide.

Oh! sad was the lot of the orphan girl,
'Mid the hurried crowd, life's busy whirl,
And oft would she think of her early days,
As they gather'd around the social blaze,
In her childhood's home, where a mother smil'd
On the happy sports of her gentle child;
 Then pause! nor with mocking words deride
 The name of a hapless suicide.

Oh! that cottage home is desolate now,
Though the leaflet blooms on the shading bough;
Hush'd, hushed is the laughing voice of mirth
That once sounded around that joyous hearth;
The parent that nightly her child had blest,
In the old church-yard is now at rest.
 But she—oh! a doating mother's pride—
 Hath fill'd the grave of a suicide.

Death hovered there with his icy hand,
And sever'd the chain of the household band,
Oh! one by one hath each form departed,
Like the autumn leaves, till, broken hearted,
She, alone desolate, was left of all
That had gather'd within the cottage hall;
 Then 'twere better she too had died,
 Nor fill'd the grave of a suicide.

Have ye never mark'd 'mid the stormy cloud,
How one star may gaze thro' its ebon shroud,
Like a lonely heart; how to earth may cling
A timid flower that still breathes of spring.
While the wintry winds sweep harshly on?
Oh! thus she drooped, like a leaflet torn
   From the parent stem, with a heart so tried,
   Alone was the hapless suicide.

Mark where the sensitive *Landon* lies,
There many a tear from kindliest eyes
May oft hallow the silent bed of earth--
There many a flower may wake to birth--
There pitying Angels may ceaseless weep,
And their Vigils through crowded years may keep,
   As fame bears on, on her glowing tide,
   The name of a hapless suicide.

Oh! ye of the glad and the joyous heart,
How little ye dream of the bitter part
That many a mortal is doomed to here—
Of the sorrowing hours, the scalding tear
That often hath wet the pillow nightly;
Then bethink, nor even speak thou lightly,
   Nor scorn the turf that doth meekly hide,
   The form of a hapless suicide.

SONG.

Oh! give me the night,
When the stars are bright,
    And the breeze sweeps gently by;
When the ripples flow,
With sparkle and glow,
    Beneath the beaming sky.

And away I'll roam,
O'er the dashing foam,
    With Ella by my side.
While flashes the stream
'Neath the moonlight's gleam,
    I'll win my bonnie bride.

And away we'll glide,
O'er the curling tide,
    While skies are glowing bright.
Oh! for love's sweet art,
To enchant the heart,
    Give me the starry night.

LEARN TO BEAR.

Learn, learn to bear,
Thy meed of care,
    The hope of joy retaining,
Though woe and strife
May cloud thy life,
    Still bear without complaining.

Ne'er turn from earth,
Nor quell thy mirth,
    Though heart from heart may sever,
'Tis vain to sigh,
When broke the tie,
    Though loos'd the bond forever.

Though word and smile,
May prove but guile,
    So ends our blissful dreamings—
They wither all—
And fade and fall,
    E'en as the meteor gleamings.

Though griefs are thine,
And thorns may twine,
    Amid hope's fairest roses,
Though earth may cloy,
From care and joy
    Life's bubbling draught composes.

Though fierce the might,
Of sorrow's blight,
   Learn! 'tis our mortal doom,
That each should share,
His world of care,
   'Ere shuts the gaping tomb.

Still meet thy part,
With cheerful heart—
   Nor pine in hapless sadness—
Some ray may gleam,
To gild life's stream,
   And wake thy soul to gladness.

FRIENDSHIP'S OFFERING.

Friendship as pure as holy tie,
   As e'er linked heart to heart,
With us ne'er let an earthly ill,
   E'er rends its bonds apart.

A friend indeed 'mid grief or joy,
   Let each be to the other,
Bound by the kindly gentle tie,
   Of sister, and of brother.

And when long years have passed away,
　How oft will mem'ry fly,
Back to the hours together spent,
　That now are rolling by.

Still let sweet friendship round our hearts,
　Her holy influence twine,
Heav'n guide you is the honest wish,
　My heart would speak to thine.

———◆———

A SUMMER SHOWER.

A song for the rain that sparkles and flashes,
That gushes, and foams, and dances and dashes;
How grateful it falls on the withering flow'rs,
As down like a torrent of jewels it show'rs:
While the little bird peeps from its covert of leaves
And the glad swallow nods in the old cottage eaves,
Still whirling, and quivering over and o'er,
In Elfin like dance the starry drops pour;
While Iris is flinging athwart the dim skies,
Her mystical wreathing of radiant dyes.
Though with it there oft o'er the mind steals a sadness
'Tis a blessing to all, a token of gladness;
Ev'ry heart in the land should greet it with pleasure,

Each sparkle a gem—each bubble a treasure,
Now glancing to earth—and now lost in the seas,
As they carrol, and laugh, and shout with the breeze,
While sporting, cascading down the green hills,
In miniature falls—pour the shivering rills;
And the field, and the lawn, late parched with heat,
All glitter and flash, as they smilingly greet
The sunbeams that peep thro' the mist that enshrouds
Now darting and gleaming—now hid in the clouds:
Ah! many will welcome the soft summer rain,
'Tis a beacon of hope to the harvesting swain,
A guerdon for toil, and he blesses his God,
As the glistening currents pour down on the sod;
For with it soon passes all boding of dearth,
And Ceres is waving her sceptre o'er earth.

FAIR THE BLOSSOMS JOY IS WREATHING.

Fair the blossoms joy is wreathing,
  'Round the hoping, trusting heart,
Where no leprous care is breathing,
  To rend the rainbow hues apart;
But fancies dim, like visioned glories,
  That cheer the soul by grief untried,
To the mind like fabled stories,
  Return when rolling years have died,
    By mem'ry lighted.

Bright they come, as in youth's blooming,
  The loved—the lost—the changed—the dead.
But a strange, unearthly glooming
  O'er each phantom memory's shed.
Ah ! all—yes, all that gleamed so bright
  Upon the soul in happier hours,
Come back, as on a winter's night,
    The moonlight glittering splendor showers
        O'er earth so blighted.

The fondly loved, the wildly cherished--
  They who, chilled in death, are sleeping,
That in youth's holy time have perished—
  Still the heart their beauty keeping,
Lips that in such truthful seeming
  Vows of love so fond have spoken;
Ah ! little dreamt ye, in hopes dreaming,
    Those vows should all be wrecked and broken,
        Earth's fearful waking.

Bitter lessons life is teaching,
  To blast the heart and sear the brain,
Soon the cheek and lip are bleaching,
  Where sorrow holds her cheerless reign;
Dream ye not, amid youth's gladness,
  All the ills that may beset,
How the heart may pine in sadness,
  O'er the joys ye can't forget,
      In anguish breaking.

THE BEGGAR.

With meagre face, and sunken eye,
  And look so sad and worn;
She wanders through the busy street,
  Till eve, from early morn.

And stopping at the rich man's door,
  She begs a crust of bread;
Then turns toward her wretched home,
  In trembling fear and dread.

The poor child pleads for charity,
  As slow she wanders on;
In hungry, hollow voice she pleads,
  And meets but look of scorn.

And ye among the heartless crowd,
  How can your hearts rejoice—
And still refuse the pittance small,
  Begg'd in suppliant voice?

Thus born in poverty and want,
  And bred 'mid crime and shame—
Till she has learned in very hate,
  To fear the rich man's name.

Oh! turn thy weary heart from earth,
  This region of unrest;
There is a brighter home for thee—
  A kingdom with the blest.

Like the summer's breath,
  Or the closing day.
Sweet spirit of earth,
  Thou hast passed away.

TO MARY.

'Twas but a dream of happiness.
  That faded with the past—
A vision—Oh ! too beautiful,
  Too heavenly to last.

And thou wert by my side, my love,
  With thy sweet, winning smile,
Which could so oft in sorrow's hour,
  My weary heart beguile.

Where art thou now, Oh ! lovely one ?
  For hope and joy hath flown;
Thou'rt cold, and still, nor hear'st my voice,
  Thou'rt gone, gone from thine own.

Thou wert too beautiful for earth,
  Too pure for earthly love;
A spirit bright of holiness,
  Call'd to its home above.

THE BROKEN VOW.

'Twas the evening chime—'twas the trysting hour,
And Adela sat in her vine wrapt bow'r,
Her heart throbbed high as she listened in vain,
For the step that never might come again;
For the knight was false to his lady fair,
Though he'd vowed by the braids of her glossy hair;
'Ere the dew should fall on the sleeping flow'r,
He'd seek her again in her elfin bower.

While she lists, lo ! the trembling leaves are stirr'd,
It is but the flight of a restless bird;
Thro' the grim twilight its fleet course winging,
The woods with its joyful notes are ringing.
But eve's first sentinel walketh the sky,
And he the lov'd Conradin, why, Oh ! why
Is he not now by the faithful side
Of her he has pledg'd as his chosen bride.

'Twas June, the rose wreathed, beauteous June,
And bright were the rays of the summer moon,
And rapid the flow of the whimp'ring stream,
As it imaged the light of each starry gleam;
But crimson the hue of her cheek deep flush'd,
And sad were the thoughts thro' her heart that gush'd,
As the orbit of night grew faint and dim,
Oh ! in anguish she wept and prayed for him.

While she's bowing the head, bending the knee,
The truant lover, where, where is he ?
Where the festal tapers brightly glow,
Where the dancers reel and the red wines flow.
'Tis there he has looked on a fairer brow,
And there again he has plighted his vow;
And vainly shall Adela watch and yearn,
For the step, that to her shall ne'er return.

THE POET'S HOURS.

When the god of storm rends the summer sky,
　　And the rocks re-echo the thunder's crash,
And the dome is red with one glittering flame,
　　And vivid the glare of the lightning's flash—
When on the blue of the heavenly sea,
　　With a spirit-like gloom and majesty,
Floats the jetty cloud, with an amber tinge,
　　Like a sable pall with a golden fringe.

Or when on gilded car the sun rolls up,
  And zephyrs burst forth from their crystal cell,
And heaven-born music falls sweet on the ear
  As the mellow tones of a silver bell.
When the last tint of day with its violet gleam,
  Sends a radiant flush on the land and stream,
And the orient sky with a flood of light,
  Yields to the shade of siderian night.

When the meek, white moon with her luminous train,
  Steals forth from the depths of the trembling sea,
And the topaz gleam from each glorious star
  Sends a wavy hue o'er the canopy;
When the dewy tears fall in pearly showers,
  On the glowing breast of the sleeping flowers,
And the mermaids come from their coral caves
  To sport with the beams on the glancing waves.

When the seraphs are chanting their evening hymn,
  And fays dance out from each flowret's cell,
And the fire-fly spreading his gauzy wing,
  Darts forth from the depths of the shadowy dell;
When the humming bird rests in sweet repose,
  'Mid the velvet leaves of the crimson rose,
And the butterfly sporting the rainbow's hue
  Flits light o'er the bell of the violet's blue.

When the nightingale wakens his mournful song
  That swells from the earth to the skies above,

And the scented air on its ambient wing,
  Wafts back the sigh of the sorrowing dove;
Oh ! these are the hours, when the poet's soul
  Bursts free from the chain of earth's dark control,
On pinions of fancy from regions of night,
  Soars 'mid the gleams of a heaven-born light.

WELCOME TO THE NEW YEAR.

The winter's swift passing away,
  We'll greet with glad hearts merry spring;
How soon it too from us will stray,
  On time's pitiless shadowy wing.

All greet the new year with a smile,
  With pleasure forsake the old friend,
Feel happy with her for awhile,
  As with hope to the future they bend.

But ever in mem'ry thou'lt dwell,
  With things that have withered and gone,
For nought in this world can dispel
  The remembrance of happiness flown.

Then away to the things that are past,
  In my heart thou art traced with a tear.
I turn from thee, faded at last,
  To welcome the happy new year.

THE DESERTED HOUSE.

'Tis midnight; on the ruin brown
The cold, round moon shines deeply down;
The waves on either shore lay there
Calm, clear and azure as the air.—*Byron.*

With tears look on that wreck of pride,
　That long deserted home;
The glad heart's music there hath died,
　For sorrow's blight hath come.

The flower of hope there wither'd lies,
　From Autumn's chilling blight,
There burning tears have dimm'd bright eyes,
　And day hath turned to night.

Within that old ancestral wall,
　Love's voice was wont to sound.
But it hath ceas'd and sorrow's thrall,
　Hath cast the spell around.

There smiles and tears, the bridal wreath,
　A deepening spell have wreath'd,
There hearts that now lay cold in death,
　'Mid hope and joy have breath'd.

There bright birds chant their sweetest lay,
　And gently flows the stream;
There stars still shine, and moonbeams play,
　But dim and chang'd they seem.

The bat, and owl, their vigils hold,
  There toad, and snail, are creeping,
The gloomy walls are damp and cold,
  As o'er the ruin weeping.

SONG.

My Bella Donna, smile again,
  Oh ! what sad thought, my love, hast thou,
When it can wake that bosom's pain ?
  What grief should cloud that lovely brow ?

My Bella Donna, smile still bright,
  Mark ye not the sunny gleaming,
And each clear orb that decks the night—
  Joy in ev'ry ray is beaming

My Bella Donna, smile once more,
  Let thy soul in joy be bounding;
See each glad wave that clasps the shore—
  Joy in ev'ry ripple sounding.

My Bella Donna, smile, still smile,
  Nor let thy heart ere droop in sadness;
Oh ! wear a mirthful look the while—
  Wake once more to joy and gladness.

ENIGMA.

It speaks forth in the tempest,
  And in the ocean's roar;
And in the tinniest ripple,
  That gushes on the shore.
It speaks forth from the mountain,
  From valley, and from hill,
In rushing of the streamlet,
  In sobbing of the rill.
'Tis shouted by the thunders,
  And warbled by the wind;
Mind owns it to the bosom,
  And bosom to the mind;
In ev'ry bird that singeth,
  In ev'ry tree and flower,
In ev'ry bud that opeth,
  Ye mark the mystic pow'r.

The minstrelsy of waters,
  And zephyrs' whispered tone
In sweet accordance blending,
  The might and mystery own;
From dawning of creation,
  From torrid to the poles,
In every beam that shineth,
  In every sphere that rolls;

In rosy face of childhood,
    And hoary locks of age;
Solve my riddle—ye who can,
    Philosopher or sage.

--------◆--------

MY BONNIE STREAM.

Flow on, flow on, my bonnie stream,
    Along thy bank of flow'rs;
The bank where I was wont to dream,
In childhood's happier hours.

Flow on, flow on and brightly glow,
    All joyously and free;
Still let thy sparkling waters flow,
    And mingle with the sea.

Flow on, flow on, each shining wave,
    Still let them curl and roll;
How blest for me they cannot lave,
    Glad mem'ries from my soul.

Flow on, flow on, with wanton glee,
    Ere earth again may bloom,
The eyes that loved to look on thee,
    May slumber in the tomb.

Flow on, flow on, my bonnie stream,
  And kiss my natal shore;
By thee the exile may not dream,
  May never wander more.

SPRING.

Oh ! rejoice, rejoice, for spring is here,
  With her sunny beams and show'rs,
And the wild birds trill from the woods again,
  And earth is wreathed in flow'rs.

Oh ! rejoice as thy frosty monarch speeds,
  And the rosy spring has birth.
No longer the child of poverty sits
  By a chill and desolate hearth.

The daisy and primrose burst to life,
  'Neath the day-god's lustrous gleams;
And the rills dance down from the rocky hills,
  And leap in the flashing streams.

While the butterfly floats on its gaudy wings,
  In the sparkling light of day.
Oh ! we'll merrily twine our flow'ry wreath,
  And crown the queen of the May.

The violet fair and the budding rose,
　We'll pluck from their shining stems,
And twine for the lovliest maiden's brow,
　A chaplet of nature's gems.

Then rejoice, rejoice, for the spring is here,
　With her sunny beams and show'rs,
And the wild birds trill from the woods again,
And the earth is wreath'd in flow'rs.

HOME AFFECTION.

Home affection—home affection,
　High and holy dower,
Ne'er meet we in thy protection,
　A fading passion flower;
Ever kind in true devotion
　Is thy hallow'd breathing,
With thy ev'ry sweet emotion
　ANGEL TRUTH is wreathing.

Words of trust and fond believing,
　Are ever echoed there;
Comes no worldly heart's deceiving,
　To fill the soul with care.
DEATH ALONE, with mournful rending,

May dim the smile of beauty;
While hope and love in truthful blending,
  Cheer the soul to duty.

Let us aye on thee relying,
  Cherish the pure feeling;
Where heart to heart in faith replying,
  Speak the soul's revealing.
As in her full translucent light,
  Breaks forth the cloudless day,
So free from ill and sorrow's blight,
  Beam on mine earthly way.

No trinket thou of priceless seeming,
  To decorate the heart;
To gleam awhile in fancy's dreaming,
  And tracelessly depart.
But true, and changeless in thy flow,
  "Exhaustless fount of love;"
Pure as the faith that Seraphs know
  In that bright realm above.

Blest unity of heart and mind,
  Where sounds the parent's blessing,
Where met by brothers' accents kind;
  Sisters fond caressing.
Though earthly griefs may oft annoy,
  'Neath its sweet protection,
What words may speak the tranquil joy,
  The BLISS OF HOME AFFECTION.

13

THE MAIDEN'S QUERY.

I wonder if there's a kindred heart for mine,
  Or if I a matchless lassie must be,
The vine round the oak doth so trustingly twine,
But each star doth in lonely glory shine,
Which fate now I wonder doth image mine?
The star, or the vine, I would like to know,
  Yet may I not into the future glance.
See! the moon in nun-like beauty doth glow,
  E'en the sun, like a bachelor elf, doth dance
On through the heaven's in kingly pride,
  So I, solitary perhaps, may stray,
Like a hermit sailing o'er life's swift tide;
  O'er perhaps my mate, e'en now he may
  Be looking for me—will he come this way,
Or turn the wrong corner by sad mistake?
  A luckless wight ever hunting for me,
Who could only of course his helpmeet make;
  And yet in the distance left far behind,
While coming and going like the restless wind,
  Vain suitors would win my heart from me;
Ah! if he'd only think to turn him back.
  Or wait a wee while till I gain his side,
He never a kindred spirit would lack,
  Until death our mortal hearts should divide;
But perchance I alone may my fate fulfill,
  Contented am I, be it good or ill.

ROUSE, MORTALS, ROUSE!

Rouse, mortals, rouse!
          Nor pine o'er earthly woes—
Grasp strength to bear,
          No matter what thy doom.
See 'mid grief's clouds
          One burning star still glows,
One quiv'ring spark,
          That lights beyond the tomb.
'Tis Faith's clear beacon,
          And to the mourning heart,
Like Angel nymph,
          Behold her spirit nears,
Bidding grief's shades,
          Like spectral fiends depart,
While glowing bright,
          Lo! form'd of sorrow's tears,
In fancy's realm,
          Hope's glitt'ring bow appears.

Then, mortals, rouse!
          Nor feebly e'er repine;
Still trust in heav'n,
          'Mid life's deceitful glare,
Oh! hope, content,
          May yet again be thine,
Tho' hearts prove false,

                Ah! why in frail despair
Or anguish bow?
                Nay, cast this thrall aside,
Grief's wearing bends,
                Nor e'er let sorrow cling,
Like phantom to thee,
                E'en tho' deceiv'd, belied,
By trusted lips,
                Still cheerful bear the sting,
Affection's change,
                And earth's deceptions bring.

SONG.

Thou call'st it love, when phantom like,
  Some form is near thee seeming;
Thou call'st it love, when one soft voice,
  Aye thrills through fancy's dreaming;
Thou call'st it love, and such thou say'st,
  Thy heart e'er feels for me;
Thou call'st it love—if it be so,
  I fear that I love thee.

Thou call'st it love, when in the heart
  One image e'er is shining;
Thou call'st it love, to meet with joy,
  To part with sad repining;

Thou call'st it love, and such thou say'st
    Thy heart e'er feels for me !
Thou call'st it love—if it be so,
    I know that I love thee.

* * *

MUSIC.

The raven night, flapping her starry pinions,
    Scatters the diamond dews upon the air,
That, falling, each its tiny sparkle flings,
    Mimicking heaven's dazzling hosts that cluster there.
In silent glory, no breath is heard, save
    The voice of sobbing waters tossing wearily,
Filling my soul, euphonious sound, with thee.

Music, high gift of heaven !
    For surely thou had'st birth
Amid Elysian bowers,
    And but wandered to this earth,
To render us less mortal,
    And fit us for that dwelling
Where from seraphic harps
    Thy grandest notes are swelling.

Alike in palace and in cottage home
    Awake the soundings of thy mystic voice;

Now from the minstrel's lips the accents come,
    Bidding the heart to sorrow or rejoice;
And now thou'rt ringing through the festive halls,
    Tuning the harp in high victorious strain;
Till on the ear the dying whispers fall,
    Rousing sweet fancies in the dreamy brain.

And to the mariner, far from kin and friend,
    With starry skies, the lisping of the sea,
With the sad tollings of his heart beats blend,
    Striking the chimes of restless memory;
Till the deep caverns of his soul are stirred,
    With magic echoes of soft minstrelsy;
Bringing again, the last, the parting word,
    And she, the day-star of his destiny.

Hark ! through the arching of cathedral aisles,
    The organ tones in solemn plaint are stealing;
Sweeping o'er the unconscious soul the while,
    Stirring the fountain of long buried feeling,
And to the guilty heart thy soft breath floats,
    Crimsoning the cheek with the deep flush of shame;
Now through the phalanx pour the clarion notes,
    Urging the soldier's heart to deeds of fame.

And through the mourner's breast the loud bursts thrill,
    Stilling the wailings of grief's doleful swell;
Like the blithe trilling of a laughing rill,
    Cheering the silence of sequestered dell;

And lo ! from childhood's lips the voice of song
  Soars up, a guiltless offering—and 'tis to them,
On, peerless heaven, thy purest gifts belong,
  While yet the soul is spotless as the gem !

> All earth is musical,
>   Doth not tiniest insect pour
> Its mite of melody ?
>   Doth not the re-echoing shore
> Reply to ocean ?
>   Are not the wavelets bounding
> With tinkling symphonies,
>   Harmonious sounding ?
> While in their beamy depths
>   The rosy shells are blending
> Mellifluous warbling,
>   And through the waters sending
> Rich strains of concord,
>   In low murmurs ringing,
> As if the Naiads
>   In sweet tone swere singing.

What though Orpheus' lyre be mute,
  Still doth its echoes chime,
Throughout all space—and but shall cease
  With the last knell of time.

> In nature's many-toned voice
> Are thy mystic revealings;

In the tempest's sad moan,
    In the thunder's loud pealings.

The rill and the rivulet chorus are keeping,
    The fountain and cataract dashing and leaping,
With the breath of the shower, and summer bird's song,
    Joins the lay of the breeze as he jostles along.

Where as the morn unseals her roseate lids,
    Her sparkling glances flush the sleepy air
With mellowing dyes, while Luna and her train
    Sink back abashed beneath the ruddy glare,
Where Sol, on his flaming chariot, leaping,
    Rolls o'er the sky that late in clouds bedight
Of sable hue, now drink his fiery breathings,
    Making the air one sea of blazing light.

Where wreathes all lovliness;
    Where the brightest flowers
Perfume the air, and earth
    Seems like to heaven, where the hours
Pass like unnoted visions;
    And the light zephyrs rove
Like ariel min'sters breathing
    Divinity and love.

Where thou hast triumphed in the Isle of Song,
    Italia! inspiring bride of art, the wand
Of beauty, exulting, waves o'er thee

Earth's paradise, lovely, gifted land !
There the famous nine their temples reared,
  There sculptor formed with life-like seeming
The senseless marble, as with genius' touch,
  There the dull canvass became gleaming
With lovliness; there from Parnassus
  Sweet poesy her rainbow wings unfurled,
And muses' lispings echoed to the world.

          Ethereal tide ! cradled
            And springing with creation,
          First seraphs quaffed, then poured thee
            To earth—a rich libation !
          Angels have cherished thee; and mortals now
            To thee, sweet minstrelsy, in homage bow.

———————◆———————

AFFECTIONS' OFFERING.

Belov'd ones, throbs each bosom still,
With home affections holy thrill,
The Mother's kindly word and smile,
Like sunbeams to the heart the while,
Return they yet—as beacon bright,
That gleams unchanging thro' the night,
Glad'ning the traveller on his way
With hopes of the returning day?

Oh! let her warnings in each breast,
Like guiding angels sleepless rest,
And point thy steps aright in life,
Free from the cank'ring boist'rous strife
Of wordly living—free from woes,
That sorrow in our pathway throws
To try the heart—still, still look back,
Across life's bright or clouded track,
To her devotion—let it be
The guiding star of destiny.
Let mem'ry aye with fondness trace,
Her treasur'd form, her gentle face,
The Mother's love, unswerving, true,
Refreshing as the early dew,
Comes to the flow'rs when parch'd with heat,
The Father's precept let them meet,
Within each soul a haven sure,
When Satan would the young heart lure
By wily arts—if sorrow's storm
Beat o'er your heads, oh true, and warm,
Let home affection be the guide,
'Mid ev'ry change whate'er betide.
Ah! dear ones we shall treasure e'er,
Each look and word forever dear,
The merry laugh, the jesting mirth,
That once made glad the social hearth.
Each, each a burning gem shall be,
To gleam in mem'ry's treasury.

Hope sings for ye her sweetest lays,
And Fancy paints the future days
In glitt'ring hues, all, all so bright,
The coming years to visions sight,
But know ye not, Hope falsely sings,
And mind ye too the elf hath wings,
And fancy cheating are her beams,
As Will-o'-wisps deluding gleams;
Yet nurse her for without her light,
Oh! life would seem eternal night,
And though Hope lead the heart astray,
Yet flings she glory on the way,
That else had been so sadly drear,
Her ditties well the spirit cheer.
In duty's path, then let her now,
Her rose wreath twine round heart and brow;
While youth is there live on in hope,
Nor 'mid life's ills despairing grope,
She bids thee look to Him above,
In trusting confidence and love.
A world is spread before youth's gaze,
Where Folly tempting oft betrays,
Where vice a robe of beauty wears,
To trap the soul in her foul snares,
And virtues garb may oft disguise,
Awhile her grim deformities;
But first companions of your youth,
Be Virtue's self, and sinless Truth,

Let Mercy every action guide,
With Charity each heart divide,
Let Malice and her demon train,
No record of existence stain;
But Faith her banner widely spread,
And o'er each path her sunlight shed;
God bless ye! is my soul's first pray'r,
And keep ye in His holy care.

------◆------

THEY MET AND PARTED.

They met and parted, as many oft have met,
To meet with smiles, to part with strange regret;
No treasur'd tone in either mind may dwell,
In neither heart hath friendship wreath'd her spell;
Each by the other must forgotten be,
Or e'en if either live in memory,
'Twill pass unheeded, but a careless thought,
Not the bright weavings by love's angel wrought.

Different the fates that rule their ways in life—
Both may be joyous or with sorrow rife;
His perhaps varied as the changeful gleam
Of Autumn twilight,—hers the thoughtful beam
That moonlight sheds.   Yet, yet I may not tell
Or question of futurity—dissolv'd the spell
That ne'er on earth shall re-united be,
Nor yet be linked beyond eternity.

TIDE OF TIME.

Lo! the tide of time is gushing
  Onward to the eternal shore,
Wave on wave is swiftly rushing,
Clouds o'er shade and sunbeams glossing,
Ev'ry ripple's hurried tossing,
  Bearing each its mighty store.

See! that tiny bark o'erladen
  With hope's fairest, gayest flow'rs;
Bears it, too, a lovely maiden?
But reckless folly guides the helm;
Soon dark griefs may overwhelm;
  A cloud above the pathway low'rs.

But who steers on that shatter'd vessel
  So fearless on its stormy course,
Where contending waters wrestle
'Mid life's every sorrow saving?
'Tis Faith! her snowy pennant waving,
  As forth she holds the holy cross.

One lone being there is kneeling,
  Worn from sorrow, wash'd from sin;
With repentant pray'r appealing
Peace unto her heart is giv'n.
Long that weary one has striv'n
  The narrow way to enter in.

But mark upon the broadest ocean
  One shallop tosses to and fro.
Mov'd by ev'ry wavelet's motion;
Intemperance hand in hand with crime,
In revel wastes God's precious time,
  'Till all too late with death they sue.

Yet watching angels strive so sadly
  The reckless heart from sin to stay,
While conscious guiltiness so madly
The demon tempter nurses ever;
The better pathway seeking never,
  Chosing alone the darken'd way.

There one haven broad outspreadeth,
  Where folly steers her course with crime;
There night eternal darkness sheddeth;
But at the narrow entrance standing
Thousand forms are brightly banding
  To worship him who guides all time.

SONG.

Come dearest to yon mountains brow,
  And twilight's beauty share,
Where sweetest flow'rs their perfume fling,
  Upon the dewy air;

Come love, oh fairest Lady come,
  True as yon star of night,
E'en as that dazzling orb pours down,
  On earth her steady light;
E'en so in changeless, faithful love,
  This heart would watch o'er thine,
Then say thou wilt be mine, dear maid,
  Then say thou wilt be mine.

Speak, Lady, speak, thou know'st the time,
  Of parting hasteth nigh,
Give but one gentle word my love,
  One look, one whisper'd sigh;
The midnight hour tolls sadly forth,
  The fairy Village bell,
We part and yet thou giv'st no sign,
  No token of farewell;
'Tis sad to break the golden links,
  Of love's bewitching chain,
And heart so true as mine, dear girl,
  May ne'er be thine again.

THE UNREQUITED.

"Breathe of deep love—a lonely vigil keeping,
  Through the night hours—o'er wasted wealth to pine,
Rich thoughts, and sad, like faded rose-leaves heaping
  In the shut heart—at once a tomb and shrine."

How often they would together rove,
  'Neath the moon's soft light of a summer eve;
Then she tried to check her girlish love,
  In sweet tones he spake—and but to deceive.

Oh ! time doth add to the quenchless flame,
  And though unrequited—yet none might trace
The why, that whene'er they breathed his name,
  Deep flushes o'erspread her youthful face.

Oh ! she knew the parting hour was near,
  And it pass'd; but naught could e'er break the spell
His words were false—yet they still were dear,
  Their last was a cold and careless farewell.

She met him again—but with such pride,
  Oh ! such scorn as woman can nobly wear;
The flow'r of hope in her heart had died,
  And she cast it from her without a tear.

He saw her queen of many a heart,
  And deeply he rued his folly the while,
It pierc'd his soul like a poison'd dart,
  As she turn'd from him with a haughty smile;

And oft they met 'mid the worldly crowd,
  In halls where the fairest and brightest move;
Not long fair Adela's spirit had bowed
  'Neath the pangs of her unrequited love.

IMMORTAL LIFE.

"Whosoever liveth and believeth in me shall never die."

This life is like a happy dream,
  Tinged with soft and rosy light;
But o'er our joys dark shadows fall,
  As day must yield to gloomy night.

Yet what will not earth's creatures bear,
  If but allowed the pow'r of breath?
What fearful visions fill our minds—
  What horror, at the thought of death!

Then search the tablet of thy heart,
  And meekly bend to heaven's control;
By penitence and righteous deeds,
  Wash out each stain from off thy soul.

And judge not thou thy fellow man—
  No matter what his fault may be;
And turn not from the erring one,
  Lest heaven, offended, turn from thee.

14

Oh ! be not won by earth's false show,
  Seek, after death, to dwell with God;
Turn from the vanities of life,
  And tread the path our Saviour trod.

CITY TOILERS.

When twilight is flinging her mantle gray,
Shrouding the beams of the golden day,
Then may ye look on the toiling mass,
As the hurrying crowds like wavelets pass;
Mark as the wearied throngs go by,
Oh there's many a lovely lip, and eye,
And many a delicate form and face,
That might the lordliest palace grace,
But their's is a life of ceaseless striving,
While the few in pamper'd state are thriving,
'Tis their's to labor, to struggle, and strive,
But to keep the vital spark alive,
The sad existence, not worth retaining,
Every nerve, and life cord straining,
But for the pittance that barely will feed,
The beggarly wants of hungry need.

From morning's light, 'till evening's dawn,
Sat a faded girl, with garments worn,
  And cheeks so wan and pale;

Speedily plying the countless stitches,
Aiding to swell another's riches.

And what to her was that hoarded wealth?
Wearing out youth, and bloom, and health,
　　Still toiling day and night,
There by the taper dismally burning,
A mite for another's welfare earning.

And there when the midnight stars were glowing,
Oh! there she sat, still sewing, sewing,
　　Weary, and sick at heart,
And paler, and paler, the wan cheeks grew
As noiselessly by the moments flew.

And moonlight was pouring its ghastly gleams,
Mocking the shadowy taper's beams,
　　Yet there the thin form sat,
Still the fingers clasped the needle and thread,
And the thin form sat—but the soul had fled.

The city toilers what pleasure have they?
In wearisome labor, from day to day;
Oh! their's alas is a way of sorrow,
What joy for them in the dawning morrow?
And what joy for them in the sunny light?
Or the sparkling beam of the starry night,
The flower clad lawn, or the flashing stream,
Though earth with a thousand beauties may teem;

Oh! what joy for them in the balmy air ?
Thus born to wrestling with world of care,
'Tis seldom that pleasure may gladden the hours,
For mirth lurketh not where poverty cowers.

> Oh! some from the light of their earliest years,
>   Are bred to labor, and strife,
> In doleful ignorance plodding along,
>   Through a dull, and irksome life;
> While with the smiles of fate still blest,
> The dronish few may idly rest.

> And what is childhood to them, forsooth ?
>   'Tis sad those innocent years,
> Should wake to the changeful ways of earth,
>   With its shrouding doubts and fears;
> What is childhood to them, forsooth ?
> Little they know of the joys of youth.

When first morn's roseate lids unclose,
Though some may wake from sweet repose,
And hail with joy the kindling blaze,
That sparkles in her radiant gaze,
To them her fairest glance is bringing,
But the anvils ceaseless ringing,
Busy hands and tireless sound,
As the hurrying wheels go round,
The flaming forge, and whirling mill,

Oh! bliss by far the soil to till,
Where soft contentment wreathes her joys,
And seldom grief the heart annoys.

Ay the butterfly throngs may idle the day,
In sinful slothfulness, while the poor, oh! they,
Must work—work, or starve, constant employment,
Must still labor, labor, without enjoyment.

Wearied and worn, and sad of heart,
To labor, and strive, tis a hapless part
To wear out health for another's weal,
That seldom one ray of pity may feel,
But too oft on the toiling throngs look down,
With a pitiless sneer or a taunting frown,
Tho' fashion may flaunt in her senseless pride,
How often a faded raiment may hide,
And the blistering thorns of poverty bind,
A purer heart, and a richer mind,
As far in the depths of earth's sombre breast,
The glittering gem may hidden rest,
As pure and spotless as an Angel giv'n,
To sanctify earth with a ray of heav'n.

By a sullen light in a dismal room,
  A wasted form lay sleeping,
And a woman was toiling 'mid the gloom,
  A hapless vigil keeping;

And her full heart heaved with many a sigh,
As the winds like madden'd fiends danced by,
   And her eyes were dim with weeping.

And ever as the solemn hours went past,
   Moment, by moment flying;
The shorten'd breath came heavy and fast,
   Still sighing,—sighing,—sighing;
For there death in triumph had set his stamp,
And the brow with his frosty dews was damp,
   The faded form was dying.

And when the evening shades were stealing,
   Their ghastly shadows weaving,
Still, still to the toiler's gaze revealing,
   The form yet gently heaving;
Like the faint swell of a waveless ocean,
'Twas the ebbing tide of life's emotion,
   The soul earths' fetters leaving.

Oh! long, long ago, she had breathed the vow,
   And her plighted faith had giv'n;
To the being who laid beside her now,
   Who through grief-fraught years had striven.
How little she dreamt in that hour of joy,
That sorrow would every hope destroy,
   And her soul e'er thus be riv'n.

Still ever she toiled and hapless wept,
    And her eyes were dim and red,
While the cherished one beside her slept,
    And her soul was filled with dread;
But morning broke o'er her boding fears.
And faster and sadder flowed her tears,
    The wasted form was dead—

Ay! the cheek may blanch, and the lip may pale,
And the heart may *wither*, the strength may fail,
'Till number'd at last with the peaceful dead,
Ah who will mourn o'er the being fled?
Not mortals—no shadow will cloud our earth,
But Angels in triumph will hail its birth,

TIME OF FLOWERS.

Thou'rt gone, thou art gone, glad time of flow'rs,
    Lost, lost in eternity;
Leaving of sad, and of blissful hours,
    A checquered memory,
              Of griefs and joys.

Thou'rt gone in thy pomp and splendor by,
    Like vision of love and truth,
Thy leaves all withered, and lifeless lie,
    As the treasur'd hopes of youth,
              Which time destroys

Thou'rt gone, as gleams of the golden day,
   May fade 'mid the storm, and cloud;
As peace may flee from our earthly way,
   And fearful sorrows enshroud,
             The yearning soul.

Though joy hath gladden'd the heart awhile,
   Grief may dim the future years;
O'er face that beam'd with a cheerful smile,
   Now the heart wrung bitter tears,
             May hapless roll.

Thou art gone, but with thee too hath fled,
   Full many a joyous dream;
Fleeting, and frail as the rich beam's shed,
   By sunlight on the stream,
             So dazzling bright.

Thou'rt gone as the spell of innocence,
   May flee from the human heart,
'Tis sad oh! earth that so oft from thence,
   Truth's holiest gems depart,
             Like fading light.

Thou'rt gone and love once fondly cherished.
   Where the heart with faith relied;
Like thy rainbow hue hath chang'd, or perish'd,
   They, we dreamt that years had tried,
             The trusted friend.

Yet thro' all,—oh! let my heart still dwell
    In its own bright world of thought;
Let not the falseness of life dispel,
    The visions by fancy wrought,
               'Let nought e'er rend,

Thou'rt gone, thou'rt gone, and many that hail'd.
    With joy thy radiant birth;
'Mid thy bloom the roseate cheek hath paled,
    And wither'd away from earth,
               Lost for evermore.

To greet thy smile, in that deathless sphere,
    Beyond the immortal skies;
Where the heart shall meet all it e'er lov'd here,
    Where truth,—beauty never dies,
               The blessed shore.

BLUSHING,

    Loveliest by far is beauty's cheek
      When tinged with the crimson hue;
    The delicate tints a soul that speak—
      Kind, innocent and true—
    A word, or a look, may start the stream
      From heart to temples rushing.
    Who loves not the modest face to view,
      Suffused in artless blushing!

Pure token, thou, of a sinless breast,
  Where kindliest virtues dwell,
Where truth and peace like angels rest,
  And wreathe their holiest spell;
Slight the emotion that wakes the tide,
  The brow of candor flushing;
Oh, the gentlest feelings of the heart
  Are told in artless blushing!

The gem may add its lustrous ray
  To adorn the outward part,
But the changeful hues of the blush's play
  Are the language of the heart;
For they tell of a mind undimm'd by vice,
  All spell of evil hushing.
Oh, who would ere doubt the guileless heart
  That speaks in artless blushing!

The colorless face, the pallid brow,
  May perhaps enchant thine eye,
But give me the cheek that owns the glow
  Of nature's healthful dye;
It seems to shadow an honest soul,
  Where the purest thoughts are gushing;
And loveliest, far, is beauty's cheek
  When tinged with artless blushing.

MARCH OF LIFE.

Marching on and marching ever,
  'Mid plenty, pestilence and starving,
Backward turning never, never;
Hearts may break, and kindred sever,
        Yet ne'er the weary race is run,
        Until eternity is won.

Cheek, and bloom, and youth are fading,
  Still whiter grow the locks of age,
Some thro' seas of anguish wading,
Griefs their souls forever lading,
        Myriad hearts with sorrow heaping,
        Bowed to wretchedness and weeping.

Rich and poor together wending,
  Strangely vice and virtue meeting,
Good and evil quaintly blending,
Soon the hurried march is ending;
        'Mid pleasure's smiles or sorrow's frown,
        The vital gift must all lay down.

Some, in folly's gaudy dressing,
  Have never known an hour of sadness,
Never felt cares' bleak distressing
Blessed with fortune's soft caressing,
        In the lap of luxury nurst,
        With no pang of misery curst.

All are hast'ning to that ocean,
  Where mortal and immortal sever,
There must end all life's emotion,
Hearts with all their fond devotion,
    Mortal spirit there must yield,
    Lip and eye forever sealed.

See! a fair and joyous being,
  Enchanted walks a way of brightness,
With no dreaming or foreseeing
That the moments from her fleeing
    Will bear away the roseate flowers
    That joy upon her pathway show'rs.

While in fancy's sunlight basking,
  We live in an ethereal world,
Yet may come the fearful tasking,
Blighted hope, and feelings masking,
    Can earth have aught to charm us more,
    When those dreaming hours are o'er ?

Ideal nympths such glories twining,
  Create a paradise within,
But the rays so brightly shining,
Fade as twilight's hues declining
    Soon thought's fairy-land is blighted.
    Fled the elves that so benighted.

Worn, and weary, and forsaken,
  One moves amid the gathering throng,
Soon her step by death's o'ertaken,
In a happier world to waken,
      Released at last from sorrow's snare,
      Eternal peace awaits her there.

Blighted one, once hope was singing
  To thee of fair and blissful hours,
O'er thy way such splendor flinging,
Gladness to thy bosom bringing,
      For that heart, what—what is left
      Of all its dearest visions reft ?

Spirit! look where quenchless burning,
  The star of faith divinely glows;
From affliction bravely turning,
Forbearance from earth's trials learning,
      And seek in that pure sphere above
      A refuge in a Saviour's love.

Shrivell'd form, and tresses hoary,
  Age's tottering steps are moving,
Faded now his dreams of glory,
Soon will end life's changeful story,
      And all its pleasures, all its pain,
      May never thrill his soul again.

Childhood too, with mind so cheerful,
  Gambols 'mid the varied throng,
Knowing not how gay or tearful,
Fate may wait them bright and fearful,
      Revelling in the dreams of youth,
      'Ere yet the soul hath known untruth.

Why should end their youthful joying ?
  Why should grief's stern spectre start them ?
Angel natures thus annoying,
Guileless happiness destroying?
      Would heav'n that they might ever be
      From care's besetting vipers free.

Marching on, life's thread is weaving,
  Still unwinds the fragile cord,
Mortals hoping, weeping, grieving,
'Mid earth's trusting and deceiving;
      'Tis well if in the hapless race.
      In one true heart ye find a place.

JUNE.

Behold the roseate June is here,
  With flowery vines and dewy gems,
With clustering buds and berries bright,
  Now pendant from their fragrant stems;
The tulip in her brilliant garb
  So proudly rears her crimson vest,
While daisy, in her modest bloom,
  Peeps timid from her grassy nest.

The varied roses droop their heads,
  Like blushing maids in coyful pride,
While orange-wreaths and lilies white
  Deck summer as a lovely bride;
And lo ! the violet so meek,
  . The peony and mignonette,
The jasmine, larkspur, daffodil,
  And she that bids us not forget.

The myrtle, telling of true love,
  And snow-drops all so fair and frail,
Narcissus, iris and sweet pea.
  And pink so delicately pale,
Carnation, grove-love and hare-bell,
  Magnolia and rich woodbine,
The passion flower, verbena pure,
  . And golden-gemmed loasa vine.

Like fairies met in rivalry
  Along the banks of every stream
Sweet flora's flower jewels now,
  In varied beauty, glorious gleam
Mocking the rainbow's heavenly dyes,
  With many a dazzling, radiant hue;
All emblems, too, of mortals, each—
  Of pride, of worth, and virtue true.

The cherries twinkle through each bough,
  All brilliant in the morning light,
While strawberries, like coral gems,
Glow temptingly upon the sight;
  The raspberries like rubies, gleam
  Amid their downy emerald leaves,
And clustering currants, thickly hang
  Where sunlight glittering fret-work weaves.

And birds their rapturous notes pour forth
  In strains of gladness on the air,
E'en as in Paradise of old,
  Ere earth had known of sin and care
The oriole's mellifluous songs
  Now rouse the drowsy early morn,
The whip-poor-will in carols soft
  Proclaims the twilight's hazy dawn.

The rills adown the mountains spun,
    And gently murmur their delight,
And fountains leaping into air,
    Sprinkle their diamond sparks of light ;
While sleepy cows with, lagging steps,
    Amid the fruitful pastures rove,
The sportive lambs in frolic wild,
    With graceful antics, playful move.

The busy ants in armies march
    To labor where the sunbeams glow ;
The merry bees, like changeful friends,
    From flower to flower haste to and fro ;
The butterfly, so languid, soars
    And flaps her wings so rich, so vain !
And locust, darting swiftly by,
    Repeats his ever whirring strain.

The healthful trees extend their arms,
    In their green robes of summer drest ;
The sloping hill, in verdant pride,
    Bears high its grassy velvet crest.
The trees, the plants, each drop of dew,
    Proclaim the great Creator's power,
Who made each star a rolling world,
    And shaped the modest daisy flower.

15

Iris her mazy pendant hangs
    Athwart the dreamy azure sky ;
While in the west the piling clouds,
    Like mimic mountains quaintly lie.
Pomona laboring with the sun,
    A store of luscious fruit will heap ;
While Ceres soon the ripening grain
    With thrifty care will plenteous reap.

Oh, woman ! turn from fashion's halls,
    Where pomp and folly warp the heart ;
Learn from the flowers this lesson true,
    That nature needs no gauds of art :
Let her sweet gifts our time employ,
    That now to vanity is given,
Then we, though clothed in mortal form,
    May show the attributes of heaven.

All hail the farmers ! men, indeed !
    The hardy tillers of the earth ;
Nature's true noblemen are they,
    Of sturdy, sure and matchless worth.
Long may the members of this club
    In wisdom meet, as they do now,
Imparting knowledge to the world—
The heroes of the soil and plough !

FANCY'S WEAVING.

All the day I sate me weaving,
   Glittering threads in loom of thought,
Nursing fond the gay deceiving,
   Fancy's cheating elves had wrought.
Sitting 'neath the old tree's shadow,
   Down beside the laughing stream,
With no thought of earthly pinings,
   Lost in vision's happy dream.

While the sunlight snake like coiling,
   Twisted with each dimpl'd wave,
As if amid the shining waters,
   Mermaids their bright tresses lave;
Far into the night still dreaming,
   Thought like wilful fairy flies,
Up to heav'n as fain 'twould pilfer
   Some bright planet from the skies.

High amid the bright world's wand'ring.
   In the azure sky above,
Hoping there some kindred spirit,
   Would give back true love for love,
Dream'd I of a heart so faithful,
   'Mid my ev'ry wo, or joy,
But I fear me 'mong life's changes,
   The real shall my sweet dream destroy,

All fair the brilliant threads were woven,
　　As bright sunbeams there were 'twin'd,
Without one shadow on their glowing,
　　So rich the mingling hues combin'd ;
So would I ever thus be weaving,
　　Glittering threads in loom of thought,
Nursing fond the gay deceiving,
　　Fancy's cheating elves had wrought.

A LAY FOR YOU AND I.

Though mighty thy sorrows to brave it e'er try,
　Tho' thy peace and thy joys, like a temple o'erthrown;
Seems scattered around, tho' care's spectre may sigh,
　O'er the happiness now that forever hath flown ;
　　　　　O'er ruin of years,
　　　　　Hope's rainbow appears,
And mercy's clear sunlight pours down from on high,
Tho' grief's tempests are hov'ring still in life's sky.

Tho' affections may change, though hearts may grow cold,
　Still, alas ! as mortality often will do,
There's one to his bosom the stricken will fold,
　There is one 'mid all trials, forever is true ;
　　　　　Then never despair,
　　　　　But trust to his care,
Who the numberless sands of the sea hath told,
No matter what woes in life's plan are enrolled.

Tho' the loved and the loving have passed from our sight,
Tho' the voice that was dearest may greet us no more,
Faith's star will shine out, thro grief's stormiest night,
Like a beacon of hope from some far distant shore ;
As still 'mid the haze
On the mariner's gaze,
A gleam from the lighthouse is glittering bright,
So faith 'mid life's shoals all the pathway shall light.

My brother, on earth I must still, still bear on,
Tho' thy love that sustained me when trials were near,
Forever like starlight from life has been shorn,
My way all so sad without thee doth appear,
The future so bright,
Is vail'd all in night.
Yet hope still is singing like lark at the dawn,
We shall meet on that shore where all cease to mourn.

Ah ! youth, all thy dreamings soon, soon must they leave,
My bosom will pine o'er their shadowless flight,
The glorious visions fair fancy can weave,
Reality, dismal and grim as the night,
May kill with a breath,
Like spirit of death,
While we o'er the past in lone sorrow may grieve,
And weep that stern time should the soul thus bereave.

Care's weary ones, why in despondency bow?
  Rouse up in life's battle, still fearless move on,
See faith rear her banner and calls to ye now,
    There's a cross to be borne—there's a prize to be won,
            Why lag in the way,
            To the endless day,
There's a glittering crown for each sainted brow,
For all who shall win in the struggle below.

Ah ! surely my brother a crown thou hast won ?
  And e'en now 'mid the Angels in glory art blest;
In splendor surpassing the noondays bright sun,
    In the light—light eternal thy spirit doth rest,
            So perfect seem'st thou,
            I dream of thee now,
On the bosom of Him who awaits to adorn,
Each spirit from earth to His presence that's borne.

Ah ! ye who, in poverty, labor and pine,
  There is peace and a guerdon that waits you above;
Thou meek one, who dauntlessly meets all that's thine,
    Oh ! thou—thou art the first in God's pitying love,
            When earth shall have passed,
            First there, tho' here last :
And seraphs for each their bright chaplet shall twine,
When ye in the kingdom of glory shall shine.

Ah ! proud child of fashion and folly take heed,
  For so narrow's the pathway that leadeth to God ;
Beware lest some demon of evil mislead
  Thy steps from the path by the penitent trod ;
            For scarce can we tell,
            If aught we do well.
As moment on moment so swiftly doth speed,
Such watching the earth bounded spirit doth need.

THE WINDS.

Whirling, careering o'er city and plain,
  In boisterous singing the wild winds are sweeping,
Like giants in strength on their tireless course ;
  Now here, and now there ever dancing and leaping ;
            Ah ! wierd minstrels are they,
            On their shadowless way.
Like phantoms hurriedly fluttering by.

O'er drear home of poverty mournfully sad,
  So doleful the sound of their spirit like singing ;
Where a weary one sits in hunger and woe,
  But death there a balm to that pain'd heart is bringing,
            For on wings of the blast,
            Lo ! the worn soul hath past,
To that griefless home in the glittering sky.

Lost in mid ocean a wreck'd bark goes down,
   Where each proud wave, on wave, is franticly bounding,
There the shivering winds their trumpeting notes,
   With the last lone sob of the dying is sounding,
          And the firmament rings
          With the sound of their wings,
As tossing and springing from wave unto wave.

'Mid the tombs that like ghastly spectres gleam out,
   A solemn dirge they are plaintively chanting ;
Like troubled souls from their earth temples cast forth,
   Now the graves of their tenantless dwelling haunting ;
          For so wierd like and strange,
          On their mystical range,
In sorrowful sighing from grave unto grave.

Ah ! many a tale could ye whisper, wild winds,
   Of guiltiness, crime, and of mortal anguish,
Of the widows and orphans who friendless sigh,
   And the myriad hearts that unpitied languish ;
          Oh ! could ye but tell,
          In your choral's swell,
Of all ye have witnessed from day to day.

Yet of many a gladsome scene could ye sing,
   Of the festival throngs in joy abiding,
Of the fond vows pledging in innocent love,
   And hearts where no serpent of sorrow is hiding ;

Yet away do ye sweep,
O'er the city and deep,
So heedless of all on your drearisome way.

No comfort ye bring, oh ! ye pitiless winds,
To the heart that aches for the lost and the loving,
For ye seem but to mock at our human woe,
As onward from palace to cot ye are roving ;
But like a spectral bell,
Ye so solemnly knell,
As if rung from the shores of eternity.

Speed by, oh ! speed by, no kind ministers are ye,
For no gladness is felt in your chilly breathing,
But of sorrow, and pain, ye seem ever to wail,
While the dun clouds for earth their snow bands are
But away with the night,   [wreathing ;
Be your hurried flight,
For ye sing but a sorrowful dirge to me.

APPEAL FOR NICARAGUA.

America, thine hand extend,
To him, the fearless and the brave,
A second Washington now asks,
Your aid to succor and to save;

Thousands down-trodden in the dust,
  By tyrant will despotic bound;
Ah! freedom, let thy beating pulse,
  Throughout each throbbing heart resound.

Walker the dauntless, lo! he shines,
  A beaming sun before the world;
And soon may Liberty's proud flag,
  By his brave spirit, be unfurled
O'er Nicaragua, gifted land,
  That now in servile bondage sighs;
Freeman, a brother's hand extend,
  Nor moveless hear oppression's cries.

Behold! as Summer's blooming queen,
  In nature's loveliest hues bedight;
She offers now a precious store
  Of luscious fruits and blossoms bright,
Columbia, view thine hapless child,
  Like captive maiden left to mourn;
Deck'd as a bride that comes to wed,
  And finds her love but met with scorn.

Oh! tear the fetters from her limbs,
  Unlink the chains that bind her now;
God gives us one to burst her bonds,
  And twine the olive round her brow.

His patriotic—gallant deeds,
   Shall blazon on the shield of fame;
And mothers teach their lisping babes
   To love and bless our Hero's name.

Arm 'gainst oppression's dastard sway,
   And Freedom! let your watchword be;
Let tyrant rule and slavish bonds,
   Give place to priceless liberty.

SONG.

Prostrate lo! I bow before thee,
Thus to woo and thus implore thee,
Lady, Oh! my heart restore me.
       Or say thou wilt be mine.

Angels bless, protect, and guide thee,
Never may an ill betide thee,
Mercy ever watch beside thee,
       Peace and joy be thine.

May I ask amid thy dreaming
Where truths holy gems are beaming
Like the stars in ocean gleaming,
       I may sometimes be.

If too much this fond heart's asking
Never more 'twill claim the tasking,
But thankful be if happy basking,
                In dreams—-in dreams of thee.

Meeting thus thy gentle glances,
Every look my heart entrances,
Every smile thy pow'r enhances,
                Treasure of my heart.

Leave thee, dearest? never—never,
Know that I am thine forever,
From thee, oh! 'twere grief to sever,
                Say not we must part.

IN MEMORY

OF ONE WHO DIED IN BLOOM OF YOUTH.

'Tis over—and the pulsing heart,
  Hath ceas'd for aye its mortal throes;
'Tis over, and the beaming eye,
  Is slumbering now in death's repose:
No more ye'll hear the merry laugh,
  With its sweet tones of gladness ring,
No more ye'll hear that gentle voice,
  The great Creator's praises sing.

Yet wherefore weep, ye would not sure
  Becall her to earth's changes now;
Nay she hath reached that better land;
  Immortal chaplets crown her brow.
Thou lovely temple of a soul, ·
  As thou art now—we all must be.
Who would not fling earth's glories down
  For the sure bliss that welcomes thee.

So young to die—in youth's fresh bloom,
  A warning sad to me, and all
Who late have marked thee sudden pass,
  As leaflets from their branches fall;
I scarce had known thee 'ere thou'dst fled,
  A minister of God's holy love,
An angel sent in mortal guise,
  To teach the path that leads above.

So much of what thou wert in life,
  In thy calm features might they trace,
Though death—the terrible—the stern,
  Laid his white shadow on thy face;
Peace to thine ashes—and thy soul,
  Oh! may it in heaven's splendor rest,
Nought—nought of earth may reach thee there,
  In that far dwelling of the blest.

OH! THERE'S A GRIEF.

Oh, there's a grief to pale the check,
  And rend the sternest heart,
When death shall come 'tween friend and kin,
  And tear love's links apart.

Thou fearful hour when Mother fond,
  Her anguish'd tears must shed,
Above her infant's precious form,
  All lifeless--pale—and dead.

My heart could bow to any ill,
  Could bear with fortunes change,
And tearless mark earth's selfish hearts,
  When careless friendships range.

But wo when those the dearly priz'd,
  No more may wander near,
When ceas'd affections gentle voice,
  With its sweet tones to cheer.

Oh! grievous agony of wo,
  The soul may know of ever,
When heart with heart so fondly link'd,
  Stern death hath forc'd to sever.

So vainly fall the bitter tears,
  When earthly ties are riv'n,
Yet turn, ch! grief wrung souls to God,
  Look up with faith to heav'n.

TO F——.

Doth friendship, the sincere, the true,
  For me dwell in thy breast?
There let it, in calm holiness,
  Like Angel spirit rest,
There let it dwell as radiant clear,
  As sunbeams glancing bright,
A holy spell—a beaming star,
  A ray of quenchless light.

Why talk of age;—'ere yet time's frost,
  In thy dark curls we trace?
Why talk of age,—ere yet his lines
  Have furrowed o'er thy face?
Why warn of worldly heartlessness
  As some strange wizard art?
Nay! let me still believe the face,
  Forever speaks the heart.

The world—I seek not to be thrown
  Amid its varying throng,
But choose in fancy's realms to live,
  A simple child of song;
Then judge them not—as artful, false,
  Who scarce the world may know,
By candor o'er life's changeful scenes,
  Truth's holy splendors throw.

BRIGHTER DAYS.

When writhing 'neath afflictions smart,
When torturing sorrows rend thy heart,
    Oh! turn thy gaze—
Not to the past, but future years,
Still hope 'mid all thine anguish'd tears,
    For brighter days.

But picture forth the coming hours,
Wreathed in fancy's richest flowers,
    And beaming rays;
Though blighting winds sweep harshly by,
Yet dream, though ev'ry leaflet die,
    Of brighter days.

Though the dear songs thou'st loved of yore,
May greet thy raptur'd ear no more,
    The thrilling lays,
  Though the loved form be cold and dead,
  Oh! hope, though ev'ry joy has fled,
    For brighter days.

Though friendship's bonds are rudely broken,
Though love hath left no treasur'd token,
    To cheer life's ways.
Though eyes once fond grew cold and strange,
Oh! dream 'mid ev'ry blight and change,
    Of brighter days.

Though no hands with love caress thee,
Though no mother's voice may bless thee,
    In words of praise;
Though fondest hearts may coldly sever,
Oh! trust 'mid darkest trials ever,
    For brighter days.

What though like sunlight from the stream,
E'en hope may lose her gladdest beam,
    Her cheerful blaze,
Ah! yet mid fearful doubt and ill,
Let happy fancy whisper still,
    Of brighter days.

Though thy heart is filled with sadness,
And never one sweet tone of gladness,
    Across it strays;
Yes! though thy soul be sorrow riv'n,
Still joyful turn to yonder heav'n,
    For brighter days.

MONODY.

Lo! romping o'er the hills so joyous,
  Dances along the merry rill,
As 'ere came sorrow to annoy us,
  The heart with gladness aye would thrill.

16

But soon its gleesome, singing, hushing,
　Comes forth the Winter's frosty breath,
And ceases then its lively rushing,
　Palsied as by sudden death,

As all so glad thou tiny river,
　Onward thy mimic wavelets flow,
While bright the sparkling ripples quiver,
　In the Summer's sunniest glow.

So she in meekest holy, trusting,
　Cheerful journeyed on life's way,
Till Death with swift and sudden thrusting,
　All sternly bade life's pulses stay.

While fondest hearts were grateful beating,
　So high with hope and thankful pray'r,
Came that spectral presence cheating,
　Of the prized—the treasur'd there.

Like a lily crushed and broken,
　All lifeless lay that slender frame;
And gave she not one farewell token,
　'Ere life had yielded its last claim.

Yet a soft, a heavenly seeming,
　Aye! made her to affection dear,
While yet of earth, the spirit gleaming,
　That told she might not linger here.

Sadden'd hearts bow down repining,
  And mortals may not yield relief;
But with quenchless, deathless twining,
  TRUE FAITH SHALL TRIUMPH OVER GRIEF.

When sorrows on the soul are preying,
  Then came our Savior's words to bless;
Still seems it that kind voice is saying,
  "I WILL NOT LEAVE YE COMFORTLESS."

Oh! never by God's love forsaken,
  Thy cross He'll give thee strength to bear;
Ah! wherefore mourn that He has taken,
  The fragile blossom to His care.

As comes the Springtime gently waking,
  The rill from Winter's frosty spell;
E'en so her soul earth's fetters breaking,
  Shall in eternal glory dwell.

CHANGING.

Thou, and I, and all are changing,
  Changing with each busy hour;
Look! throughout earth's varied ranging,
  The shell upon the wave-beat shore,
  How soon Time steals the gleam it wore;
Naught may 'scape the ruthless power,
From human heart to the simplest flow'r.

Affection, too, is gaily roving,
   Forever seeking a new charm;
For those we dreamt so fondly loving,
   She's rang for aye her funeral knell,
   They stand apart by some weird spell,
That vain we struggle to disarm.

They so kind, so soon forgetting,
   Ah! change, thou blaster of the heart;
Like Simoon hopelessly besetting,
   Destroying in thy wayward train,
   Hope's buds that may not bloom again,
When rent the shudd'ring leaves apart.

Eyes that, in their star-like gleaming,
   Seemed to light our earthly way;
Too oft we find it all but seeming,
   Love's sunlight—dreamt we once their glow,
  'Till wak'd in agony to know,
That treach'ry lurk'd beneath their ray.

New born hopes to life upstarting,
   O'er wreck of those that just have fled,
Sorrow's frenzied spectre darting
   Her fiery arrows through the breast,
   That peace and joy so late have blest,
And sweet content her rainbow spread.

Changing mortal to immortal,
  A blessed holy thought in this;
For those who strive to gain heav'ns portal,
  'Mid all the struggling, burning throes,
  Of earth and its embitter'd woes;
To know tho' here our life's amiss,
Beyond there is a world of bliss.

A HYMN.

Jesus, my Saviour, guide and aid
  Me in the path aright,
Be Thy dear word to me portrayed,
  By heav'n sent truthful light.

When I Thy holy Scriptures read,
  Cast the dark vail away
That I with knowledge may take heed,
  ' And all its truth survey,

Teach me Thy law to love and keep,
  And Satan's snares to shun,
Teach me to watch, and not to sleep,
  'Till all Thy will be done.

Thou know'st, my God, without Thy pow'r,
  I could not conquer sin,

For Satan tempts thro' every hour,
  My soul from Thee to win.

Then Jesus, Saviour, leave me ne'er,
  But love and succor me,
If I, like Peter, faithless fear,
  Stretch forth Thine hand to me.

------◆------

A PRAYER.

Another year, another year,
  Hath leaped into the eternal sea,
And in that year most gracious God !
  How have I serv'd or worshipp'd Thee ?
Teach me Thy bless'd commands to keep,
  My heart from pride and folly win;
Oh ! Saviour, with Thy cheering love,
  Take from my soul all thought of sin.

And those I love, Redeemer bless'd,
  Direct their hearts in virtue's way,
By Satan's dark deluding wiles,
  Let them not, Lord, be led astray.
In Thee, my God, I hope, and trust,
  Oh! Father, guide our hearts aright,
Until we stand redeem'd and pure,
  In that bright world of endless light,

DREAM ON.

Dream on, dream on, oh! doting heart,
  Full soon may come thy waking,
To know how earthly joys depart,
  To feel thy life cords breaking.

Dream on, dream on of future hours,
  No thought of grief divining,
Yet thorns are nestling 'mid hope's flow'rs
  That round thy heart are twining.

Dream on, dream on of priceless truth,
  Each honied word believing,
Full soon shall wake thy sunny youth,
  To feel earth's sad deceiving.

Dream on, dream on in innocence,
  Nor start the dark revealing,
That yet must rouse thine eve'ry sense,
  To weep o'er slighted feeling,

Dream on, dream on of changeless love,
  Of heart to heart united,
Thou'lt wake to know how hearts can rove,
  To feel existence blighted.

Dream on, dream on, each glance still prize,
  Bestowed in artless seeming,
Thou'lt wake at least 'mid tears and sighs,
  To know thou wert but dreaming.

TO MY MOTHER.

Oh! sound thee, my harp, thy holiest lay,
To her who is pure as the sunny ray,
That falls on the earth in a golden show'r,
From the eastern sky, at the morning hour;
When nature awakes from her dewy repose,
As the bud bursts forth to a blushing rose.
My mother, oh! pure as the liquid beam,
That Cynthia pours on the crystal stream,
'Mid waste of the desert—a jewel bright,
That gleams like a star thro' the misty night;
Or lily that bows, as the wild winds pass,
Its virgin head 'mid the silken grass;
Not fleeting thy love, as the zephyrs sigh,
Or meteor's course through the dome on high;
Or the transient gleam of an April day,
Or the sparkling change of the diamond's ray;
Fix'd in my heart doth thine image lie,
As the polar star, in the northern sky,
Oh! bright as the tinge, like a gorgeous bow,
On a purple cloud at the sunset glow;
My mother, my father, with each gentle word,
What a gushing fount in my heart is stirr'd;
What a joyous thrill thro' my bosom's sent,
With glorious hallowing mem'ries blent,
Of my childhood's home, of those golden hours,
When life seem'd a twining of richest flow'rs,

When our hearts were gay as the laughing spring,
And our songs were glad as the wild birds sing;
Thou'st guarded us mother, thro' trials and fears,
Thou'st smil'd with our smiles, and wept with our tears,
Shield her, oh! Father let my heart warm pray'r,
Soar from this region of death and despair,
To thy temple of peace—that home of the blest,
Where sorrow will end and the soul be at rest.

THE BETROTHED.

The sun fast sought his ev'ning rest,
  Tinging nature with golden ray;
While o'er the earth, brown shadows play'd,
  As warning of the closing day:
And then appear'd eve's first lone star,
  Bidding night claim his weary round,
Of dark and dreary solitude,
  When all are in sweet slumber bound;
There's clarion notes borne on the breeze—
  Proudly wave's each warrior's plume—
Those daring hearts but pant for fame,
  Nor dream they of their coming doom.
And Albert breath'd a kind farewell,
  And bade each doubt and fear depart;
But there was sadness in his voice—

That boded ill to Lila's heart;
He clasp'd her fondly to his breast—
  Then nimbly mounts his gallant steed,
And oft turned back with eager gaze,
  As through the moonlight on he'd speed.
Then, as she ponder'd o'er the past,
  From her beauteous soft dark eye
Freely flowed the pearly tear;
  And from her bosom burst a sigh,
Seeming to bid a sad farewell
  To ev'ry bright and joyous scene,
Where they in love's soft, moonlight hour
  Had oft, so oft together been.
But then she check'd her burning tears,
  And strove to stay the wild unrest;
That, like the ocean's troubled wave,
  Swell'd high within her gentle breast.

  (How frail are all the rosy wreaths
    That hope twines round the youthful heart;
  We little dream of their decay,
    Till one by one the flow'rs depart.)

And there came one—but all unmeet,
  To linger in that heart's sunlight—
A shadow on its surface clear—
  A cloud where all was fair and bright.
He sought to win her—not with smiles—

But to her selfish father turn'd,
  With tender vow, and promise fair,
    Till that sire with proud ambition burn'd.
Yet, 'mid the dance, and at the feast,
  Still Lila wore a happy smile;
None would have dreamt, to see that face,
  The woe that rent her heart the while.
Her step was light—her songs were gay,
  As in the golden days gone by;
But the bright eye, and paling cheek,
  Told that the fatal hour was nigh!
For o'er that brow, so marble white,
  Now sorrow cast a deep'ning shade,
As 'neath the cold and bleak north wind,
  The brightest flow'rs of earth will fade.
No rose hue tinges that soft cheek,
  No ling'ring of youths sunny day;
It were not well for this sweet face
  To lose its wonted cheerful ray,
No friend was near, to cheer that heart,
  No kindly mother's voice was there;
That gentle one had breath'd for thee
  Her dying, last, and fervent pray'r;
That sire had look'd into that eye,
  Where death its gloomy spell reveal'd;
Kneeling beside that couch of pain,
  He vow'd his child to guide and shield,
From all the ills that might assail,

Or ruffle her life's changing stream;
But from his mind that hour had past,
  As fades the mem'ry of a dream.

It suited ill—that gorgeous scene—
  Or sumptuous bridal feast;
The bitter thoughts, and breaking heart,
  That struggled in poor Lila's breast.
And, Albert, did not heav'n forewarn
  Thee—of the scene enacted now?
The bridal robe—The snowy wreath—
  That deck'd thine own betrothed's brow?
And little thought those happy guests,
  While gazing on that simple wreath,
Of hopes, that like the stagnant stream,
  Lay dormant in the heart beneath.

    (Oh! woman—thou weak fragile thing—
      How much in life hast thou to bear!
    For ever, in thy cup of joy,
      There's sure to fall one bitter tear.)

To Albert, far from Briton's coast,
  News came, ere yet the month had sped,
His lady, though still true to him,
  Would be unto another wed.
The battle o'er, in triumph now,
  To his dear home he quickly hied;

With anxious heart he spurs them on,
  To tear her from a rival's side.

The bridegroom now, with haughty mien,
  Led forth his pale and trembling bride;
That daughter sacrificed, to feed
  A father's vain, ambitious pride,
Like lily 'fore the sacred shrine,
  The fair dejected Lila knelt,
'The tear suppress'd; the smother'd sigh,
  Hid what that throbbing bosom felt.
The vow scarce breath'd, ere from the throng
  Albert, with palid, anxious face,
Stepp'd forth—ah! well she knew that form,
  And swooning sinks in his embrace.
Oh! long he gaz'd on that fair brow,
  And eager lists return of breath;
Fondly he kiss'd her o'er and o'er,
  But Lila's lips were cold in death!

And rosy morn stole slowly forth,
  Flinging her blushes o'er the earth;
While nature, with sweet harmony,
  Welcom'd with joy her cloudless birth.
But where was she, the fair betroth'd?
  A holy silence dwells around;
'That lip has ceas'd its murmer low—
  Hush'd, hush'd, is ev'ry mirthful sound.

(Oh! death, there's beauty in thy pow'r,
  Which all of this bright earth must feel;
The bliss of an immortal life,
  To all mankind thou dost reveal.)

Ay! cast aside the bridal robe,
  And bring the shroud—the pall—the bier—
The eye that late with triumph beam'd,
  Is darken'd now by sorrows tear;
Old sire! weep on! well may'st thou weep
  O'er thy pale victim, cold and still!
Look through thy tears, and see her there,
  The reed that bow'd to thy stern will;
And Albert, oh! thou, too, must weep;
  Thy vows, thy pray's, are all in vain;
Not tears, nor sighs, nor earthly pow'r,
  May bring thy Lila back again.

  (How oft, too late—too late we pour,
    O'er vanish'd hopes our burning tears—
  O er darken'd dreams, that once were bright;
    The shadows from departed years.)

Oh! thou art sad! and Lila's lute
  May wake for the no joyous strain;
No more—no more—thoul't hear that voice,
  Till heav'n unites your hearts again.
Albert, now bow'd in heart and mind,

For loos'd were love's endearing bands,
He left his home, where all was dark,
   And sought for change in distant lands,
But that stern father, where is he?
   Behold him in yon lonely cell—
A maniac!—for when Lila died,
   Beneath the stroke his reason fell.
'Tis o'er! and I have told my tale.
   Not as the mighty bard would tell;
Lena, to thee I raise my strain,
   To Lila's memory—farewell!

———◆———

OUR EARLIER YEARS.

'Tis mem'ry strikes her mystic harp,
   To sing of other days;
And lo ! the voices of the past,
   Chaunt forth their spirit lays;
Warbling of brighter, happier hours,
   'Ere yet the heart could dream;
How transients was the meteor blaze,
   That lit life's changeful stream.

Oh ! love, and hope, how false your light,
   How fleet, and false your stay;
Too soon the clouds of sorrow chase

Your sunbeams from our way;
And what is life? to some a dream,
  A path of rosy light;
To others oft eternal gloom,
  A black and starless night.

The past, the sad, the happy past,
  Comes floating on my brain,
As on the parching summer flow'rs,
  Pours down the sparkling rain,
Comes back the scenes of childhood,
  My mother's gentle smile,
Ye blessed hours of infancy,
  How thoughts of ye beguile;
'Ere ruthless time with wizard breath,
Hath warn'd the heart of change and death.

The heart at most is a wayward thing,
Though in it the purest affections spring;
'Tis *changimg*--the lover may idly rove,
Yet nought is so true as a mother's love,
We may trace it back thro' the by-gone years,
To our careless sports and our childish fears,
To the kiss oft pressed on the thoughtless brow,
Is there aught in this world so holy now?

Then nature spoke to the heart—from rock and hill,
From the woodland shade and the sparkling rill,
From flowery fields, and flashing streams,

Oh ! *youth* is a *fairy world of dreams,*
But they fade, like the rainbow tints away,
Or the golden beams of the closing day;
And ne'er may the future, one joy restore,
Like the peace enshrined in our hearts of yore.

How blest are they—the youthful throng,
   The merry hearted child;
It hath no dream of sadness yet,
   No sorrow deep and wild;
For *griefless* are our early tears
To those that *fall* in *after years.*

Oh ! weep not o'er the early dead,
   The guiltless one at rest;
When the gaze is fixed—and the brow is cold,
   And the white shroud wraps the breast,
What—tho' the form lies 'neath the sod,
   The sinless spirit hath past to God.

And chide thou not the youthful heart,
   Oh ! check not its wild glee;
Though its sweet tones of merriment,
   Bring no glad thoughts to thee;
Still let its songs of joy be loud,
Though thy heart be lone in sorrow bow'd.

Oh! hallow'd time of innocence
   How doth the soul repine;

O'er the bright visions fled with thee,
  Those blissful hours of thine,
And mem'ry turns the giddy brain,
  To live your *beauties* o'er again.

--- ◆ ---

JEANIE.

Where Teviots dale an' waters meet,
The waves come dancin' to your feet,
Wi' voice o' music laigh an' sweet.

There ance o' eld dwelt lassie braw,
As ever graced a Scottish ha',
Wi' sparklin e'en an' brow o' snaw:

Proud Donald strove to win her saul,
But owre it he had na control,
Than owre the pearls the seas that roll.

The winsome maid wa'd na'e relent;
She cou'd na'e wi' a heart content
To be his bride e'er gi' consent:

For Willie was the lad she loo'd,
He vainly to her had na sued,
But won the cantie lass he woo'd:

An' how her heart wad heave an' swell,
As tales o' faithfu' lov he'd tell,
O' a' its magic witchin' spell.

'Twas e'en—and brightly blink'd each star,
While Cynthia on her glintin car,
Row'd on in majestie afar;

The sea nymphs sported wi' the waves,
While elfies darted frae their caves,
Like moonlight gleamin' owre the graves;

The saft win's wi' the foliage play'd,
While neath the hawthorn's flow'rie shade
Sat Willie wi' the bashfu' maid;

An' there the lovers a' sae true,
Kiss'd owre an' owre a sweet adieu,
While nae a care their bosoms knew;

An' as he clasp'd her to his heart
Alake! she was sae laith to part,
The vera thought her soul wad smart:

There mony a vow he'd breath'd sae kind,
An' mony a wreath sae braw he'd twin'd,
Wi' hawthorn an' wi' rose combin'd;

As light he scrambled owre the hill,
Whare wanders doun the sabbin' rill
The lee lang day wi' plaintive trill;

Sae aft he cried, fareweel, my love;
While echo frae the rocks above
Still murmur'd back, fareweel, my love.

Her heart was sairly sad an' lane;
For ere a fleetin' year had gane,
An' ere the twelve month moon shou'd wane;

Her minnie bad, wi' stern command',
Her wed the laird o' mickle lan',
An' link her fate in Hymen's ban'.

'Twas simmer—an' the win's sae frae,
Still gamboll'd on wi' wanton glee,
Owre hill and dell, owre flow'r and tree;

The birdies sported 'mang the heather
An' bobb'd and blink'd at ane anither,
And sang sae cheerfully thegither.

An' as the gloamin' glimmerin's fade,
Owre mount an' dell, owre burn and glade,
In ilka rainbow hue and shade.

Puir Jeanie strayed wi' heart sae wearie,
Whare last she parted frae her dearie,
Aneath the hawthorn now sae drearie—

That rose beside the flow'rie hill,
Where wanders doun the wimplin' rill,
The lee lang day wi' plaintive trill.

The morrow came wi' golden ray,
An' a the world look'd glad an' gay,
As joyfu' for her weddin' day:

Though frae her cheek the rose had died,
They led her to the kirk wi' pride,
To mak' her there stern Donald's bride.

They reck'd nae o' her wild despair,
While a' the shaw and grandeur there
But fill'd her faithfu' heart wi' care.

They ca'd her love a youthfu' dream,
Like rays o' starlight owre the stream,
That flee an' lea'e na ling'rin' gleam;

Or meteor frae the brow o' night,
Whas beam may lea'e na trace o' light,
Where a' was beautifu' and bright.

But 'mid the minnie's doatin' pride,
Just ere they ca'd the lass a bride,
Young Willie bounded to her side:

Then Donald's look was sair dismayed,
As the fond lover clasped the maid,
To find his drauchit scheme betray'd.

Ance mair rang out the marriage bell;
An' louder still hits peals wa'd swell,
As gif the joyfu' tale to tell.

An' ne'er a bonnier bride, I ween,
In a' the wide, wide warld was seen,
In village lass or courtly Queen.

An' mony a gleefu' heart was there,
To greet wi smiles the happy pair;
Wha wa'd nae in the triumph share
O' ane sae beautifu' an' fair ?
Joy shouted in the vera air,
        An' echo laugh'd wi' glee.

FLORA'S DEPARTURE.

Swift, swift, see the delicate summer is passing,
  Like an angel of beauty and mirth,
On the breath of the flowers she wingeth her flight,
  And now Autumn reigns sov'reign on earth;
Still, the proud hills are wearing their emerald robes,
  While laughing forth in the sun's jeweled ray,
The ripe fruits are shining, but earth's blooms fading,
  Silently fading by leaflets away.

Oh, 'tis sad that the grave, e'en the fairest should hide—
  Sad a cloudlet should darken the sky—
Oh, 'tis sad that earth's spirit like flowers should fade —
  "Sad the beautiful ever should die."
Yet, there's blight in the blast as it sweeps o'er the cliffs,
  As it sports with the old forest tree,
Oh, there's blight in the blast as it moans through the vale,
  Like the voice of the storm howling sea.

While like dewy wing'd sprites in the glittering air,
  The fountain's clear waters are leaping,
Though still gorgeous and bright in the westerly sky
  The sunset's rich colors are heaping.
Oh, but paler and paler the tyrian dyes
  Through twilight's dim hazing is streaming,
Like the hectic that flushes on beauty's soft cheek,
  Still fainter and shadowy gleaming.

And no daisies are strewing the death-blighted sod—
    There no wild buds or violets peep,
But still Zephyr is singing her lullaby song,
    As if hymning loved summer to sleep.
Pomona is guarding her ambrosial gems,
    As old Time numbers out the swift hours,
While all crownless and sad, lo ! sweet Flora departs,
    With a girdle of withering flowers.

A SIGH TO THE PAST.

A sigh to the past—to the future a smile,
    Whate'er it may be, still the present is ours;
Though clouds may have shadow'd life's sun for awhile,
    And sorrow hath wither'd hope's loveliest flow'rs,
Yet ne'er weep o'er the gems once lost in time's sea,
    Nor look to the future with doubt and decay,
For the present is ours, whate'er it may be,
    If peace is thy guest, be content while ye may.

For ye may not recall one moment of time,
    Adieu to the past—know for aye it must sleep,
Though mem'ry shall oft wake her mystical chime,
    And thought o'er the byegone its vigil shall keep;
The old year hath died—and time's pinions unfold,
    Still bringing us nearer and nearer the tomb,
Ere another long year shall its records have told,
    Oh! what shall awake from futurity's gloom?

MEMORIES.

Oh! wind, thou dirge-like, dismal wind,
 But whisper of the past—
Of the things that were—the music flown,
 The tones that could not last—
      But died away.

From that vista dim, there's sad return
 Of strains once soft and clear—
Of the tones that fled, like the passing breeze,
 And left no echo here—
      No ling'ring lay.

The sad—the glorious past —that went,
 Like the early breath of spring;
The notes that burst from the shatter'd harp,
 On the last unbroken string—
      The wild deep note.

It wafts me echoes of joys that past,
 Strains of my native land;
Sweet voices, that once could glad my soul,
 Of the scatter'd household band—
      Around me float.

And music, that came like the mournful tone,
　Of a young bride's fun'ral knell;
From hearts, oh! sad as the captive's heart,
　'Mid gloom of his starless cell—
　　　　　　　The thrilling tone.

It wafts me the roar of the gushing sea,
　The song of the summer guest;
And the sigh—that emblem of hidden grief—
　Born of the heart's unrest—
　　　　　　　Deep sorrow's moan.

It brings me the last enchanting word,
　That died on love's soft breath;
It murmurs of joy, of birds and flow'rs,
　Of sorrow, pain and death;
　　　　　　　Of things unkind.

Then cease, thou dirge-like, dismal wind—
　Roll back, thou tide of years;
The bitter fount—the mingling false,
　Of joy, and sorrow's tears;
　　　　　　　Take back, oh! wind.

OH! WHY IN SADNESS BOW THE HEAD.

Oh! why in sadness bow the head,
  O'er blighted hopes the heart bereaving;
Oh! there are woes o'er which to shed
  Thy tears in true and earnest grieving;
Go to the home where sorrow flings
  A damp on every hour of living—
Where poverty like Banshee clings—
  To scenes like this thy tears be giving.

Ungrateful child of wealth and ease,
  And pamper'd state, forever wanting
Some whim or wish, wherewith to please
  Thy selfish heart—while care is haunting
Thy neighbor's steps, while he lone sighs,
  In hungry wretchedness repining;
No fancied grief his bosom tries—
  But yet for him a beam is shining,

Brighter than aught that earth can give—
  Faith, faith, that weary heart is blessing;
Deathless, through every ill to live,
  And nerve his soul thro' all distressing,
A lesson learn thou, too, from him,
  To bear in patience every trial,
Nor sigh o'er every falling whim,
  But teach thy nature self-denial.

TO MY SISTER, ON HER BRIDAL DAY.

Farewell! if ever fondest prayer
  For other's weal avail'd on high,
Mine will not all be lost in air,
  But waft thy name beyond the sky.
                              BYRON.

My Sister, thou must leave us now,
  Must leave thy childhood's happy home,
Thou'st link'd thy fate to one thou lovest,
  With him alone thro' life to roam.

The orange wreath that decks thy hair,
  On this thy joyous bridal day,
Be emblem of thine after life—
  Of love that ne'r may know decay,

The sparkling depths of those dark eyes,
  May tear of sorrow ne'er o'ershade
The deep'ning color of thy cheek,
  Oh! may it never, never fade.

Pure as the dew that falls at even!
  Still gush the spring within thy heart,
Of changeless love, that lives undimm'd—
  Although perhaps—for years we part.

May fortune gild thy future way,
  And Heaven crown thee with the blest,

And never may an earthly care
  Awake thy gentle soul's unrest.

Yes! go, my sister, fare thee well,
  Oh! in these words there's much of pain,
'Tis hard to part with one we love—
  Nor know that we may meet again.

TWILIGHT.

Hail! twilight hour, when the enraptur'd breeze,
Sweeps with rich music thro' the waving trees;
And the bright waters rushing on the shore,
Laugh as they dash their glit'ring jewel store
Of shining ripples, sparkling in the ray,
That sunset lends to guild the ling'ring day;
When rainbow hues in mazy splendor gleam,
Flooding the lea, and quiv'ring on the stream;
As day, enamour'd of the beauteous earth,
Blushing departs—and paling heav'n gives birth
To the first herald of night's blazing train,
That beams and flutters o'er the bounding main,
Then smiling fancy wings her radiant flight,
And pond'ring reason trims her flick'ring light;
Oh! then into the dreamy mind will steal,

Sweet thoughts and visions—then the heart doth feel,
A mystic yearning after things more high,
Then cling to earth—a wish to pierce the sky;
Then—then, if e'er the trembling soul would flee,
And fearless dart into eternity,
But for one glimpse of that unseen—unknown,
Where shine the blessed—round the Omniscient throne;
Whose pow'r inimitable we mortals trace,
In ev'ry orb that whirls thro' trackless space,
In ev'ry leaflet springing from the sod,
All bear thine impress—oh! Eternal God.
Then flushing memory will haply stray,
Back to the scenes of youth's enchanted day!
E'er the young heart had dreamed of grief or pain,
Oh! blissful time that ne'er may come again;
Alas! how little think we, then, the strife,
The many ills that cloud our human life.
But twilight hour, thou bring'st a thrilling calm,
To the worn soul—a soothing, holy balm,
That bids us lift our stricken hearts to heav'n,
Where grief shall end--and all shall be forgiv'n.

FAREWELL TO THEE, JERSEY.

When the winds are rocking the waves to sleep,
  While from rose tipped shells—like a zephyr's sigh,
Or a wind harp's moan—to the billowy deep,
  The mermaids are chanting their lullaby.
When Summer in beauty is wrapping the land,
  And flowers are gemming the emerald heath,
When the fairy queen, with her glittering band,
  Are twining by moonlight their mystical wreath;
When all earth is glad, and my heart is gay,
  Then fancy, on pinions all light and free,
Will again return—for as sun to the day,
  This heart, oh! fair Jersey, will wander to thee.

Farewell to thee, Jersey, I'll think of thee often,
  When the proud moon in splendor is shining afar,
And thought of thee still shall life's weary way soften,
  Thy memory will live in each glorious star.
I'll think of thee, Jersey, when lingering twilight,
  In shadowy beauty is gilding the stream;
When the rosy day fading gives place to the night,
  Oh! thy mem'ry shall cheer me, in waking or dream.

'Twill live in each season, in the sun's laughing rays,
  In the winds, in the waves, in the breath of the flow'rs,
And when the songsters of Summer pour forth their sweet
        lays,
  'Twill mind me of thee—and life's happiest hours.
I'll think of thee, ever, when night's orbs have faded,

And morning first beam is kissing the lea;
As nature awakes from the gloom that o'ershaded,
  I'll think of *thee, Jersey*—I'll think then of thee.

When the June, with her wreaths and her roses, shall come,
  Or bleak, leafless Autumn, with withering blast,
I'll think of thee, Jersey—of thee and my home--
  And in fancy I'll wander, 'mid scenes of the past;
For I love the glad waters that lave thy dear shore—
  Thy hill, dell, and vale, and thy soft balmy air;
And though I may rove on thy banks never more,
  I'll love thee, for oh! my sweet home—it was there.

(Where the willows are chaunting in glee to the breeze,
  That whispers each tone to the snowy-wreathed spray—
Where the landscape is stretching far out to the seas,
  That sparkle like gems in the flashing of day.)
How from thee, alas! could I ever depart—
  For the cold-hearted worldling to desecrate thee;
Yet I may not return to the home of my heart,
  Though a thousand sweet memories still bind thee to me,
Not a soft note of music e'er falls on mine ear,
  But thrills to my soul like a voice from the past
Of the hopes that have faded—the things that were dear—
  Oh! those hours, too precious--too blessed to last;
Ere time had o'ershadowed my mother's sweet smile,
  Where faith, like a ray from yon heaven, reposes,
When the fairy-winged hours passed lightly the while,
  And life seemed a Spring-time—a pathway of roses.

When at evening my sire would join in the throng,
   And glad tones of music so joyous would ring,
And the young heart was gay, 'mid the dance and the song--
   But *change* o'er that spot now a shadow doth fling.

But again--perhaps often—our fair bark may glide,
   In spirit-like beauty, o'er Hudson's dark waves,
As Elfin light skimming the breast of the tide—
   That floats on in splendor o'er glittering caves.

Oh! Jersey, I love thee—though sorrow's deep shade
   Has darkened thy light, like a spell from the tomb,
Yet this shadow may pass, as the storm-cloud will fade—
   When the rainbow is bursting, like hope thro' the gloom.

Though I go 'mid the scenes of splendor and pride,
   And in the bright revel will oft share a part,
Yet still I will turn to the years that have died—
   Still mem'ry's sweet blossoms shall circle my heart.

Then farewell to thee, Jersey—thy frown or thy smile —
   No more shall I list to thy soft vesper bell;
With sorrow I leave thee, my beautiful Isle,
And weep as I murmur, this parting farewell!

18

SONG.

Did ye greet nane, when anither,
　Had tane thy Jeanie lass awa;
Was it not sair grief to anither
　Luv for ane sae leal and braw,
Ken'd she little o' thy looing,
　That your heart was a' her ain,
Sair had been her waeful ruing,
　To hae gien anither pain.

Nae coquettish freaks were in her,
　Ay, sae meek and kind was she,
Joyfu' heart that ance cou'd win her,
　His ain wifie true to be;
Innocence the gift o' heaven,
　Dwells sae faithful in her breast;
Ane to whom her luv was giv'n,
　Weel might thoct himsel richt blest.

WOMAN'S WRONGS.

Oh! woman, thine's a weary lot—
So oft forsaken and forgot,
And left defenceless in this world
To venom'd malice, at thee hurl'd,

With none to soothe thy grief-worn heart,
Nor aid thee in thy troubled part;
To droop, neglected and alone--
Crushed the fond heart—the lofty throne
Of purity, that lovely spring.
Treated as 'twere a worthless thing.
When beauty fades from off thy face,
Or thou hast lost thy winning grace,
Man heeds not, in his wild career,
The paling cheek—the falling tear,—
By him like worthless weed cast by,
To bear thy wrongs, and bearing, die;
Nor soothes he thy last parting breath,
Nor weeps he o'er thee cold in death:
And when thou'rt wrapt in shroud and pall—
He revels in the festive hall,
And turns with fiendish art again,
Some other guileless heart to chain.
Oh! woman, would that thou couldst hide
Thy feeling heart by woman's pride;
Hide, hide thy grief by seeming mirth,
That man may estimate thy worth;
Then his the part to sue and plead,
And his the shattered heart to bleed,
And his the tear—the deep-drawn sigh—
When meeting coldness from the eye
That once could with such kindness beam,—
The sleepless night, or fearful dream.
Oh! act awhile man's selfish part,

And veil the jewel, woman's heart;
Let him but bear what thou hast borne—
The cruel taunt, the look of scorn,
Think, would he bear such woe the while,
And wear the same kind, loving smile ?
No! woman, 'tis alone thy doom,
To pass in sorrow to the tomb.

THE HEART.

Heaven ordains that each should feel,
  His share of sorrow and distress;
But this must end—and man will pass
  From ills that cling to earthliness.

Where the thorn and weeds are growing,
  There roses may not bloom;
And joy may never warm the heart,
  Where sorrow leaves its gloom.

And how oft, when storms are raging,
  The stream its bank o'erflows;
And oft the heart is flooded o'er
  With maddening grief and woes.

How oft, amid the worldly throng,
  The bright'st smiles of gladness
Are but the veil to hide the heart—
  Fill'd with woe and sadness.

How blest is he whose feelings gush,
  Free as the crystal spring;
How bright hope's flow'rs, within the heart,
  That ne'er felt sorrow's sting.

But wretched is that man, whose heart
  Is dark with crime and shame;
Oh! curst is he who ne'er hath felt
  The warmth of virtue's flame.

THE SOLDIER'S LOVE.

The purple clouds lie in the west,
  Tinged with the sunset's golden hue;
The lily holds her fair face up,
  Bathed in the twilight's shining dew.

The bleating sheep with busy feet,
  Haste at the sound of herdsman's cry,
The brooding cows in drowsy mood,
  Amid the tall grass nodding lie.

And in the deep woods solemn isle,
   Norman with her he loved so true;
Knelt by the gleaming brooklet's edge,
   There, there loves trysting to renew.

Hand clasped in hand, cheek pressed to cheek,
   So bow'd they by the brooklet's side,
Like phantoms in the shining stream,
   Shone back their faces from its tide.

But ere the warning knell of time,
   Had toll'd another twilight's end;
Norman in freedom's daring ranks,
   Went forth his country to defend.

No tidings came through weary months,
   And Norman, Ah! why came he not?
White grew the hapless maiden's cheek,
   Dreaming that trysting vow forgot.

Ah! knew she not 'mid battle's rage,
   Her lover met a soldier's death,
And dying 'mid the din of war,
   Had blest her with his latest breath.

And still at twilight's haunted hour,
   She wanders to the brooklet's side;
Like spectre kneeling lowly down,
   Her white face imaged in its tide.

TO MISS CATHARINE HAYES.

Lo! Tara's Harp awakes once more,
   A skillful minstrel sweeps the strings;
And now on Freedom's blessed shore,
   The *gifted* " *Swan* of Erin sings:
Her's the magic, rapturous strain,
To thrill the soul with joy, or pain.

On ærial wings each soft breath floats,
   Music's majestic art revealing;
O'er human hearts—the searching notes,
   Touching the inmost chords of feeling;
Blessed be the land that gave thee birth,
VICTORIOUS SONGSTRESS of the earth.

Seraphic tones—as listening—lo!
   What strange allurement charms the soul;
Earth seems a Heav'n, as in full flow,
   The chiming numbers sweetly roll,
And thou, *triumphant Queen* of Song,
The *highest* '*mid* the *angel* throng,

Apollo aside his Lyre, would fling,
   To list'n thy enchanted breathing,
Immortals choicest tributes bring;
   Thy sinless way with glory wreathing;
While proudly waves the flag of fame,
Emblazon'd with thy *lauded* name.

MONODY.

We bow Omniscient, to thy mighty will,
That calmed the winds—and bade the waves be still !
Thou'st ta'en thine own, a spirit pure and bright,
To dwell with thee, within those realms of life;
To hymn thy praises 'mid the holy trains,
That fills the skies with sweet seraphic strains.
Oh, type of him—the Saviour of the earth,
Christ, the immortal child of heav'nly birth;
Thou, thou, too beautiful to linger here,
Art happy now—in yonder brighter sphere.
Ah ! yes, thou'rt blest—for angel wings unfurl'd,
Have borne thy soul to that mysterious world;
Oh ! gem, ethereal—rose bud—spirit flown;
In vain the mother fond would clasp her own.
The cherub fair—the timid, bright eyed dove,
That sweetly nestled 'neath her shelt'ring love;
That fairy thing, her little baby boy,
Bereft of thee, her hope, her only joy;
In vain she listens for the bird-like trill,
That gave the heart such joyous rapturous thrill,
In vain she turns, elate with hope the while,
To greet the sunshine of thine infant smile;
But sorrow comes where joy so oft hath blest,
And gloom and sadness fill her lonely breast;
And those clear orbs that beam'd with such delight,
Now, now are closed, as day fades into night;

And ceas'd the beating of that guileless heart,
Alas ! 'tis hard with one so dear to part;
The deepest pang that mortal e'er may know,
Oh ! fearful blight, oh ! wretched hour of woe,
The wildest grief a mother's heart e'er prov'd,
When cold in death, the thing so fondly lov'd—
That silent woe, the tongue may never speak,
While tears of anguish course her pallid cheek,
As on the violets trembling dew-drops lie,
Like diamond-star or tear from angel's eye.
As darken'd waters o'er bright caverns roll,
So thou, oh ! grief, thou chast'ner of the soul,
Com'st o'er the heart—entwin'd with hope's fair wreath,
That still must bloom amid thy blighting breath;
The cloud floats onward—and days' golden light,
Bursts gently forth—magnificently bright,
With zephyr's soft and balmy chrystal rain,
The Summer comes—and nature blooms again;
The simplest plant lifts up its tiny head,
And lives anew—as will our blessed dead.
All, all must fade, the beautiful, the fair,
The flowers that flings its fragrance on the air;
But oh ! there's hope, though all we cherish die,
That we shall meet in homes beyond the sky,
For all that's mortal 'mid this scene of strife,
Will pass unto a brighter, holier life.
Then weep not, weep not, o'er the wreck of death,
For borne upon a trembling whisper'd breath,
As sunset gilds with many a gorgeous ray,

Of rainbow-dyes the ling'ring light of day,
That soul went forth to the celestial land,
'Mid shouts of triumph from an angel band;
Like gleams of moonlight bursting o'er the streams,
It woke to bliss—'mid Paradisean gleams;
The God of mercy from his glorious throne,
Hath call'd thy babe, hath taken back his own.
Then weep not, weep not, o'er earth's tie that's riv'n
It forms a link for thee, in yonder heav'n.

THE LAKE OF THE CLIFF.

The fire fly lamps all brightly glow,
And the owlet cries with voice of woe,
And Elfins peep from their sparkling caves;
While starlight imaged in the waves,
Sends o'er the stream a mystic light,
That lends a glory to the night;
And joyfully oh ! away we glide,
Across the silent—voiceless tide,
With cheerful hearts, and gleesome song;
That echo trembling would prolong,
That now from cliff to cliff doth bound,
And on the mimic mounts resound.
Amid thy vale of birds and flow'rs !
Oh ! blithesome pass the summer hours;

The heart so full of joy and mirth,
Scarce dreams that grief can cloud the earth.
The wild rose and the violet blow,
And the daisy lifts its brow of snow,
Upon the margin of the stream,
Where moonlight pours its silvery gleam;
While mid the grandeur of the wood,
With its deep mournful solitude,
Like gushing fount the fragrant breeze !
Makes music with the whisp'ring trees,
And morning comes with voice of glee,
While dances on so light and free;
Adown fair Chester's rocky hills,
The tiny, shouting, sparkling rills;
While sunshine lends its flashing ray,
And glitters on the brow of day;
And wild birds their soft murmurs wake,
Around sweet Chester's fairy lake.

SONG.

Thou art changed, thou'rt changed since last we met,
On thy brow care's with'ring stamp is set;
Thou art changed—on the gay and thoughtless mien,
The seal of cankering grief is seen.
In thy once glad breast, what bleak despair,
Hath placed its blistering signet there ?

Thou art changed, thou'rt changed thy hopeful heart,
In sorrow bows—and tear drops start,
From eyes where once so joyous, so bright,
Gleam out the rays of mirth's quiv'ring light,
Tell me beloved, I pray thee tell?
What power hath worked this blasting spell?

INEZ.

Within Toledo's halls there's sounds of mirth,
   And golden harps from out the walls are sounding;
Wild bursts of music—echoing soft and clear,
   In joyful cadence with the zephyrs blending;
But jealous heart marks Inez' witching glance,
Which rests on one proud form, amid the dance.

In vain Alphonzo sought her smile to win,
   And breath'd of love in accent soft and low;
In vain he sought to tempt with gems and gold,
   Oh ! not for him the blush that ting'd her brow;
But still he lingers by her side the while,
Like cloud o'ershadowing, Luna's brightest smile.

The lips compress'd speak but of smother'd rage,
   His dark eyes with a demon hate now glow;
But how unmeet with that sweet winning smile,

Is the stern frown that lingers on his brow,
As he sees fair Inez, with all woman's pride,
Welcome again Francisco to her side.

And from the scene of vanity and pomp,
  He wander'd forth, 'mid balmy breeze of e'vn,
Striving to still the passions of his soul;
  But thou, oh ! Inez, thou wert not forgiv'n;
.E'en as dark mountain sudden flames with fire,
So from his heart bursts forth the vengeful ire.

The cold, pale moon, glides on through azure seas,
  And glist'ning star-beams, trembling, kiss the earth,
All hearts are glad, Alphonzo, all but thine;
  All hearts are filled with music, love and mirth;
The wakeful night bird breathes sweet carols there,
And perfum'd rose breaths scent the mellow air.

Like the wild sweeping of the winds and waves,
  Or the fierce battl'ng of the tempests rage;
Were the dark passions that inflam'd his breast,
  Nor could reflection his mad grief assuage;
He seeks thy heart's blood—Inez, thou, so kind,
And fearful visions float throughout his mind.

And unsuspecting, onward still they move,
  Seek not, enraptur'd pair, yon tempting grove;
Some spirit seems to lure them—ev'ry sense
  Is charm'd, entranc'd, by honied words of love;

Is that a footstep—or the sporting breeze,
Wandering gaily through the whisp'ring trees?

They near the bow'r—her eyes are sparkling bright,
  And her soft cheek with struggling blushes warm,
Joyous as bird the cruel marksman's aim;
  That flits from bough to bough, nor dreams of harm;
But fierce Alphonzo, vows ere flies the night,
Their mingling souls shall greet the realms of light.

He clasps the steel he thinks will reach her heart,
  That must the beating of her pulses stay;
Wildly he gazes on the shining blade,
  O'er which the laughing moon-beams sport and play,
He hears their voices in sweet music blending,
On spirit wings to yon blue dome ascending.

And unappeas'd he seeks for vengeance now,
  Dark are the thoughts that in his bosom start;
E'en as the met'or flashing bursts from heav'n,
  So virtue's flame hath fled that guilty heart;
And brightly still glides on Guad'ana's wave,
He heeds it not, dark passions blinded slave.

And forth he springs, a dagger gleams in air,
  Then swift descends, a sudden shriek—a start;
But Inez lives ! Francisco, shielding her,
  Receives the weapon in his faithful heart;
Deeming thee slain, Alphonzo pierc'd his breast,
Then pass'd forever—that foul soul unblest.

'Twas midnight—and upon each murm'ring breeze
    Came a sweet voice in tones of deepest feeling;
Like the lone Philomel the sad notes swell,
    While moon-beams through the open casement stealing
A mournful beauty thro' her chamber sending,
With her wild dirge for the dear dead one blending.

The silver moon is beaming bright,
    Upon the glassy wave,
Melting in soft shadowy light,
    Above thy lonely grave;
And there blooms upon that holy spot,
The simple flower, 'forget-me-not!'

Forget thee! thou in memory,
    With youth's bright scenes must blend,
Thou that wert ever dear to me;
    My first—my early friend:
Light of my soul, my fond bosom's pride,
How have I lov'd thee—yet hast thou died!

I gaze upon our fav'rite star,
    And feel that thou art there,
Looking from that bright home afar,
    On me in my despair;
Star of my destiny—joy of my heart,
How have 1 worship'd thee thus—thus to part.

Will not the anguish of my heart,
   Rend the veil round mercy's throne?
Let me but wander where thou art,
   My blest one—oh ! my own;
Let the dark shadow of this life fly past,
Make me, all heavens—blest with thee at last.

The soft sweet lay had ceas'd--her maids attend,
   She bids them quick unbind her raven hair,
And then depart--but still they loiter round,
   Striving by turns to soothe her wild despair;
She thrusts them back--and with her snowy hand,
Still waves them from her, with a proud command.

The music died--but still the breeze went on,
   And from her eyes the burning tears were streaming;
Like rayless gems, their lustre all had flown;
   But now they close--and calm as infant dreaming,
She seems to rest; death o'er her spreads its wing,
They find her there--crush'd like a flow'r in spring.

And morn breaks softly o'er the eastern hill,
   On starry pinions dim night hastes away,
Lifting his sable mantle from o'er earth;
   Bright heav'n gives welcome to the crimson day
That steps forth, blushing like a timid maid,
That slow approaches as departs the shade.

Phœbus like a warrior then burst forth,
  His golden beams o'er hill and valley flying;
Till lovely evening like a spectre bride,
  Glides slowly on with gentle zephyrs sighing;
Luna looks down on vale and mountains height,
Bathing all earth in floods of silver light.

Mysterious is this change, oh ! heaven,
  Of time, of seasons, morn, noon-night's long reign;
So like the feelings of the human heart,
  Exquisite bliss—-or tort'ring care and pain;
The fond heart's treasure's love, and hope and joy !
Delusive hope, that tempts but to destroy.

In Toledo's halls—-mournful vigils kept,
  O'er the pale victim of the dismal tomb?
Her star hath set—-the lone dove is at rest,
  A rosebud blighted in its early bloom;
And thro' the dimness of the solemn night,
The flick'ring tapers send unearthly light.

Passion and crime, oh ! ye are fearful things,
  O'er ye the Angels' tears in torrents flow;
But man regards not, in his imp'ous rage,
  High heaven's commands-death chills the fairest brow;
On earth the monument then rears its head,
And all's forgotten—God will judge the dead.

19

THE BROKEN HEART.

There's a soft sweet tone in thy voice 'minds me of one
Who from this dreary earth long since did part—
One who fondly loved—'twas unrequited love—
And she hath died—died of a broken heart.

'Twas on a calm—a beaut'ous summer eve—she died,
Like that on which they parted years ago,
When he had gone—to mingle with the wordly crowd—
While she in solitude must nurse her woe.

But where, oh! where was he: upon this fatal eve?
Kneeling, perhaps, at other fair one's shrine;
And was there no sad memory within that heart?
Cherish'd he not one look—one tone of thine?

And cold in death she lay—that being once so fair—
E'en like a snow drop on her gloomy bier;
And there was many a heart that mourned for her—
O'er her affection wept its heartfelt tear.

Now with slow and solemn step they moved along,
And ev'ry heart was full of pain and gloom;
Gently they laid her in the cold—the cold damp earth,
And plac'd one snow white rose upon her tomb.

It was an emblem true of her pure spotless soul;
For she was pure as the bright dew of ev'n;
That guileless heart just felt the first fond gush of youth—
Then turn'd in sorrow to its native heav'n.

THE LAST VIGIL.

Eve's hour hath come, but brings no rest to thee—
Thou hapless mourner—while all earth is sleeping:
Why sitt'st thou there, with wild and fixed gaze,
Pale cheek, and quiv'ring lip—why art thou weeping.
And o'er thy boy this mournful vigil keeping?

Why linger here amid this awful gloom,
While all earth slumbers—youth, innocence and crime?
On, ever onward, flows the rippling sea,
And so must thou unheeding all—all, oh! Time,
As tolls the midnight hour a distant chime.

In darkness and alone, why art thou here,
Oh! fragile mourner, and seeks't thou not to rest?
Thou art not alone—the dead are near;
'Tis death thou'st clasped, fond mother, to thy breast,
Nor seem'st to know thy boy is with the blest.

Like a lone star, 'mid the gloom she lingers,
While the dim night the earth's with dewdrops steeping—
That voice hath hush'd its low sorrowing tone,
The mother's eye hath ceased its mournful weeping,
And night its vigil o'er the dead was keeping.

I DREAMED OF THEE.

I dreamed of thee—of thee I dreamed,
  Oh spirit, pure and bright,
I saw thee, fair and beautiful,
  In visions of the night;
Oh, thou cam'st so kindly to me,
  I seem to feel it now,
The pressure of thy cold—cold lips,
  Upon my burning brow.
How fondly then my spirit yearn'd,
  With thee to pass away;
And yet the tear within thine eye,
  Bade me—for thy sake—stay.
How could they ever dream of guile,
  In so good, so kind a heart?
But earth's sorrows may not reach thee,
  My blest one, where thou art;
And I will linger here, my love,
  Will linger here awhile,
For the sweet—the cheering solace,
  Of thy angelic smile.